KNOW YOUR GOVERNMENT

The Department of State

| UNION OF SOVIET SOCIALIST REPUBLICS | UNITED STATES OF AMERICA |

KNOW YOUR GOVERNMENT

The Department of State

Carl F. Bartz

CHELSEA HOUSE PUBLISHERS

ST. PHILIP'S COLLEGE LIBRARY

On the cover: Top: In 1987, Soviet Foreign Minister Eduard Shevardnadze (left) and Secretary of State George Schultz (right) sign a U.S.-Soviet agreement to hold a summit in Washington to negotiate arms control. Left: Former secretary of state Henry Kissinger (left) and Egypt's president Anwar el-Sadat meet at the White House in 1978 to discuss peace negotiations during the Arab-Israeli conflict. Right: In November 1979, Iranian militants seize the U.S. Embassy in Tehran.

Chelsea House Publishers
Editor-in-Chief: Nancy Toff
Executive Editor: Remmel T. Nunn
Managing Editor: Karyn Gullen Browne
Copy Chief: Juliann Barbato
Picture Editor: Adrian G. Allen
Art Director: Maria Epes
Manufacturing Manager: Gerald Levine

Know Your Government
Senior Editor: Kathy Kuhtz

Staff for THE DEPARTMENT OF STATE
Associate Editor: Pierre Hauser
Assistant Editor: Gillian Bucky
Copy Editor: Karen Hammonds
Deputy Copy Chief: Ellen Scordato
Editorial Assistant: Theodore Keyes
Picture Researcher: Dixon and Turner Research Associates
Assistant Art Director: Laurie Jewell
Designer: Noreen M. Lamb
Production Coordinator: Joseph Romano

Copyright © 1989 by Chelsea House Publishers, a division of Main Line Book Co. All rights reserved. Printed and bound in the United States of America.

First Printing

1 3 5 7 9 8 6 4 2

Library of Congress Cataloging-in-Publication Data

Bartz, Carl.
　The Department of State.
　Bibliography: p.
　Includes index.　1. United States. Dept. of State—History.　2. United States—Foreign relations administration.
I.Title.
JX 1706.A4　1988　　353.1'09　　88-10860
ISBN 0-87754-846-3

CONTENTS

Introduction 7
1 Keeper of the Great Seal 15
2 Diplomacy and American Independence 19
3 The Age of Free Security 37
4 From World Power to Superpower 47
5 In Washington: What the State Department Does 71
6 Overseas: What American Embassies and
   Consulates Do 93
7 Practicing an Inexact Science in an Untidy World 105
Organizational Chart Department of State 110
Glossary 112
Selected References 114
Index 115

KNOW YOUR GOVERNMENT

The American Red Cross
The Bureau of Indian Affairs
The Central Intelligence Agency
The Commission on Civil Rights
The Department of Agriculture
The Department of the Air Force
The Department of the Army
The Department of Commerce
The Department of Defense
The Department of Education
The Department of Energy
The Department of Health and Human Services
The Department of Housing and Urban Development
The Department of the Interior
The Department of Justice
The Department of Labor
The Department of the Navy
The Department of State
The Department of Transportation
The Department of the Treasury
The Drug Enforcement Administration
The Environmental Protection Agency
The Equal Employment Opportunities Commission
The Federal Aviation Administration
The Federal Bureau of Investigation
The Federal Communications Commission
The Federal Government: How it Works
The Federal Reserve System
The Federal Trade Commission
The Food and Drug Administration
The Forest Service
The House of Representatives
The Immigration and Naturalization Service
The Internal Revenue Service
The Library of Congress
The National Aeronautics and Space Administration
The National Archives and Records Administration
The National Foundation on the Arts and Humanities
The National Park Service
The National Science Foundation
The Nuclear Regulatory Commission
The Peace Corps
The Presidency
The Public Health Service
The Securities and Exchange Commission
The Senate
The Small Business Administration
The Smithsonian
The Supreme Court
The Tennessee Valley Authority
The U.S. Arms Control and Disarmament Agency
The U.S. Coast Guard
The U.S. Constitution
The U.S. Fish and Wildlife Service
The U.S. Information Agency
The U.S. Marine Corps
The U.S. Mint
The U.S. Postal Service
The U.S. Secret Service
The Veterans Administration

CHELSEA HOUSE PUBLISHERS

INTRODUCTION

Government: Crises of Confidence

Arthur M. Schlesinger, jr.

From the start, Americans have regarded their government with a mixture of reliance and mistrust. The men who founded the republic did not doubt the indispensability of government. "If men were angels," observed the 51st Federalist Paper, "no government would be necessary." But men are not angels. Because human beings are subject to wicked as well as to noble impulses, government was deemed essential to assure freedom and order.

At the same time, the American revolutionaries knew that government could also become a source of injury and oppression. The men who gathered in Philadelphia in 1787 to write the Constitution therefore had two purposes in mind. They wanted to establish a strong central authority and to limit that central authority's capacity to abuse its power.

To prevent the abuse of power, the Founding Fathers wrote two basic principles into the new Constitution. The principle of federalism divided power between the state governments and the central authority. The principle of the separation of powers subdivided the central authority itself into three branches—the executive, the legislative, and the judiciary—so that "each may be a check on the other." The *Know Your Government* series focuses on the major executive departments and agencies in these branches of the federal government.

The Constitution did not plan the executive branch in any detail. After vesting the executive power in the president, it assumed the existence of "executive departments" without specifying what these departments should be. Congress began defining their functions in 1789 by creating the Departments of State, Treasury, and War. The secretaries in charge of these departments made up President Washington's first cabinet. Congress also provided for a legal officer, and President Washington soon invited the attorney general, as he was called, to attend cabinet meetings. As need required, Congress created more executive departments.

Setting up the cabinet was only the first step in organizing the American state. With almost no guidance from the Constitution, President Washington, seconded by Alexander Hamilton, his brilliant secretary of the treasury, equipped the infant republic with a working administrative structure. The Federalists believed in both executive energy and executive accountability and set high standards for public appointments. The Jeffersonian opposition had less faith in strong government and preferred local government to the central authority. But when Jefferson himself became president in 1801, although he set out to change the direction of policy, he found no reason to alter the framework the Federalists had erected.

By 1801 there were about 3,000 federal civilian employees in a nation of a little more than 5 million people. Growth in territory and population steadily enlarged national responsibilities. Thirty years later, when Jackson was president, there were more than 11,000 government workers in a nation of 13 million. The federal establishment was increasing at a faster rate than the population.

Jackson's presidency brought significant changes in the federal service. He believed that the executive branch contained too many officials who saw their jobs as "species of property" and as "a means of promoting individual interest." Against the idea of a permanent service based on life tenure, Jackson argued for the periodic redistribution of federal offices, contending that this was the democratic way and that official duties could be made "so plain and simple that men of intelligence may readily qualify themselves for their performance." He called this policy rotation-in-office. His opponents called it the spoils system.

In fact, partisan legend exaggerated the extent of Jackson's removals. More than 80 percent of federal officeholders retained their jobs. Jackson discharged no larger a proportion of government workers than Jefferson had done a generation earlier. But the rise in these years of mass political parties gave federal patronage new importance as a means of building the party and of rewarding activists. Jackson's successors were less restrained in the distribution of spoils. As the federal establishment grew—to nearly 40,000 by 1861—the politicization of the public service excited increasing concern.

After the Civil War the spoils system became a major political issue. High-minded men condemned it as the root of all political evil. The spoilsmen, said the British commentator James Bryce, "have distorted and depraved the mechanism of politics." Patronage, by giving jobs to unqualified, incompetent, and dishonest persons, lowered the standards of public service and nourished corrupt political machines. Office-seekers pursued presidents and cabinet secretaries without mercy. "Patronage," said Ulysses S. Grant after his presidency, "is the bane of the presidential office." "Every time I appoint someone to office," said another political leader, "I make a hundred enemies and one ingrate." George William Curtis, the president of the National Civil Service Reform League, summed up the indictment. He said,

> The theory which perverts public trusts into party spoils, making public employment dependent upon personal favor and not on proved merit, necessarily ruins the self-respect of public employees, destroys the function of party in a republic, prostitutes elections into a desperate strife for personal profit, and degrades the national character by lowering the moral tone and standard of the country.

The object of civil service reform was to promote efficiency and honesty in the public service and to bring about the ethical regeneration of public life. Over bitter opposition from politicians, the reformers in 1883 passed the Pendleton Act, establishing a bipartisan Civil Service Commission, competitive examinations, and appointment on merit. The Pendleton Act also gave the president authority to extend by executive order the number of "classified" jobs—that is, jobs subject to the merit system. The act applied initially only to about 14,000 of the more than 100,000 federal positions. But by the end of the 19th century 40 percent of federal jobs had moved into the classified category.

Civil service reform was in part a response to the growing complexity of American life. As society grew more organized and problems more technical, official duties were no longer so plain and simple that any person of intelligence could perform them. In public service, as in other areas, the all-round man was yielding ground to the expert, the amateur to the professional. The excesses of the spoils system thus provoked the counter-ideal of scientific public administration, separate from politics and, as far as possible, insulated against it.

The cult of the expert, however, had its own excesses. The idea that administration could be divorced from policy was an illusion. And in the realm of policy, the expert, however much segregated from partisan politics, can never attain perfect objectivity. He remains the prisoner of his own set of values. It is these values rather than technical expertise that determine fundamental judgments of public policy. To turn over such judgments to experts, moreover, would be to abandon democracy itself; for in a democracy final decisions must be made by the people and their elected representatives. "The business of the expert," the British political scientist Harold Laski rightly said, "is to be on tap and not on top."

Politics, however, were deeply ingrained in American folkways. This meant intermittent tension between the presidential government, elected every four years by the people, and the permanent government, which saw presidents come and go while it went on forever. Sometimes the permanent government knew better than its political masters; sometimes it opposed or sabotaged valuable new initiatives. In the end a strong president with effective cabinet secretaries could make the permanent government responsive to presidential purpose, but it was often an exasperating struggle.

The struggle within the executive branch was less important, however, than the growing impatience with bureaucracy in society as a whole. The 20th century saw a considerable expansion of the federal establishment. The Great Depression and the New Deal led the national government to take on a variety of new responsibilities. The New Deal extended the federal regulatory apparatus. By 1940, in a nation of 130 million people, the number of federal workers for the first time passed the 1 million mark. The Second World War brought federal civilian employment to 3.8 million in 1945. With peace, the federal establishment declined to around 2 million by 1950. Then growth resumed, reaching 2.8 million by the 1980s.

The New Deal years saw rising criticism of "big government" and "bureaucracy." Businessmen resented federal regulation. Conservatives worried about the impact of paternalistic government on individual self-reliance, on community responsibility, and on economic and personal freedom. The nation in effect renewed the old debate between Hamilton and Jefferson in the early republic, although with an ironic exchange of positions. For the Hamiltonian constituency, the "rich and well-born," once the advocate of affirmative government, now condemned government intervention, while the Jeffersonian constituency, the plain people, once the advocate of a weak central government and of states' rights, now favored government intervention.

In the 1980s, with the presidency of Ronald Reagan, the debate has burst out with unusual intensity. According to conservatives, government intervention abridges liberty, stifles enterprise, and is inefficient, wasteful, and arbitrary. It disturbs the harmony of the self-adjusting market and creates worse troubles than it solves. Get government off our backs, according to the popular cliché, and our problems will solve themselves. When government is necessary, let it be at the local level, close to the people. Above all, stop the inexorable growth of the federal government.

In fact, for all the talk about the "swollen" and "bloated" bureaucracy, the federal establishment has not been growing as inexorably as many Americans seem to believe. In 1949, it consisted of 2.1 million people. Thirty years later, while the country had grown by 70 million, the federal force had grown only by 750,000. Federal workers were a smaller percentage of the population in 1985 than they were in 1955—or in 1940. The federal establishment, in short, has not kept pace with population growth. Moreover, national defense and the postal service account for 60 percent of federal employment.

Why then the widespread idea about the remorseless growth of government? It is partly because in the 1960s the national government assumed new and intrusive functions: affirmative action in civil rights, environmental protection, safety and health in the workplace, community organization, legal aid to the poor. Although this enlargement of the federal regulatory role was accompanied by marked growth in the size of government on all levels, the expansion has taken place primarily in state and local government. Whereas the federal force increased by only 27 percent in the 30 years after 1950, the state and local government force increased by an astonishing 212 percent.

Despite the statistics, the conviction flourishes in some minds that the national government is a steadily growing behemoth swallowing up the liberties of the people. The foes of Washington prefer local government, feeling it is closer to the people and therefore allegedly more responsive to popular needs. Obviously there is a great deal to be said for settling local questions locally. But local government is characteristically the government of the locally powerful. Historically, the way the locally powerless have won their human and constitutional rights has often been through appeal to the national government. The national government has vindicated racial justice against local bigotry, defended the Bill of Rights against local vigilantism, and protected natural resources against local greed. It has civilized industry and secured the rights of labor organizations. Had the states' rights creed prevailed, there would perhaps still be slavery in the United States.

The national authority, far from diminishing the individual, has given most Americans more personal dignity and liberty than ever before. The individual freedoms destroyed by the increase in national authority have been in the main the freedom to deny black Americans their rights as citizens; the freedom to put small children to work in mills and immigrants in sweatshops; the freedom to pay starvation wages, require barbarous working hours, and permit squalid working conditions; the freedom to deceive in the sale of goods and securities; the freedom to pollute the environment—all freedoms that, one supposes, a civilized nation can readily do without.

"Statements are made," said President John F. Kennedy in 1963, "labelling the Federal Government an outsider, an intruder, an adversary. . . . The United States Government is not a stranger or not an enemy. It is the people of fifty states joining in a national effort. . . . Only a great national effort by a great people working together can explore the mysteries of space, harvest the products at the bottom of the ocean, and mobilize the human, natural, and material resources of our lands."

So an old debate continues. However, Americans are of two minds. When pollsters ask large, spacious questions—Do you think government has become too involved in your lives? Do you think government should stop regulating business?—a sizable majority opposes big government. But when asked specific questions about the practical work of government—Do you favor social security? unemployment compensation? Medicare? health and safety standards in factories? environmental protection? government guarantee of jobs for everyone seeking employment? price and wage controls when inflation threatens?—a sizable majority approves of intervention.

In general, Americans do not want less government. What they want is more efficient government. They want government to do a better job. For a time in the 1970s, with Vietnam and Watergate, Americans lost confidence in the national government. In 1964, more than three-quarters of those polled had thought the national government could be trusted to do right most of the time. By 1980 only one-quarter was prepared to offer such trust. But by 1984 trust in the federal government to manage national affairs had climbed back to 45 percent.

Bureaucracy is a term of abuse. But it is impossible to run any large organization, whether public or private, without a bureaucracy's division of labor and hierarchy of authority. And we live in a world of large organizations. Without bureaucracy modern society would collapse. The problem is not to abolish bureaucracy, but to make it flexible, efficient, and capable of innovation.

Two hundred years after the drafting of the Constitution, Americans still regard government with a mixture of reliance and mistrust—a good combination. Mistrust is the best way to keep government reliable. Informed criticism is the means of correcting governmental inefficiency, incompetence, and arbitrariness; that is, of best enabling government to play its essential role. For without government, we cannot attain the goals of the Founding Fathers. Without an understanding of government, we cannot have the informed criticism that makes government do the job right. It is the duty of every American citizen to know our government—which is what this series is all about.

The Great Seal of the United States is used to certify the authenticity of government documents. Since 1789, the seal has been in the custody of the State Department, the oldest and highest-ranking federal department.

ONE

Keeper of the Great Seal

In an exhibition hall in Washington, D.C., stands a mahogany cabinet that houses the Great Seal of the United States. An antique stamp bearing a raised symbolic emblem, the great seal is impressed upon government documents to certify their authority. One side of the emblem pictures the American bald eagle clutching in its claws an olive branch and arrows and supporting on its chest a shield with 13 alternating red and white stripes that represent the original states. Above the eagle's head is a constellation of stars, and in its mouth is a banner with the Latin motto *E Pluribus Unum* (Out of many, one)—referring to the unification of several states into one nation. The reverse side of the emblem depicts a pyramid, topped by an eye (a sign of good luck), labeled with the date of the Declaration of Independence (1776), and surrounded by two Latin mottoes—*Annuit Coeptis* (He [God] has smiled on our undertakings) and *Novos Ordo Seclorum* (A new order of the ages). It is a design that most Americans recognize, because it is on the back of every one-dollar bill.

The exhibition hall in Washington belongs to the Department of State. Since its foundation in September 1789, the department has been the custodian of the seal. The emblem was given to the first secretary of state, Thomas Jefferson, and has become a symbolic expression of State's status as the federal government's senior executive department and one that emphasizes its role as the guardian of the nation's safety. Though not intended by the designers, the seal's symbols suggested many facets of the department's role. The olive branch and arrows suggested the department's responsibility—as the executive department in charge of conducting foreign relations—for avoiding war. The pyramid stood for the strength and stability of the nation, which the department was to foster through diplomacy. The constellation of stars represented a new state taking its place among other nations. In the nation's early years, the seal was impressed upon almost every document issued in the name of the United States. Today it is used only to seal treaties, other international agreements, and commissions of ambassadors, cabinet officers, foreign service officers, and certain other federal officials. Still, it remains in the hands of the Department of State, an important symbol of the department's preeminent role in American government.

Expressed in general terms, the Department of State's current purpose is to guide American foreign policy according to the direction of the president. The department negotiates treaties, promotes foreign trade, and represents the United States in international organizations such as the United Nations. It runs the nation's overseas missions—embassies, which handle government-to-government relations, and consulates, which handle business relations and provide public services. It supervises the Foreign Service, an organization of career officers who fill the majority of diplomatic positions. Through these foreign representatives, the department conducts day-to-day relations with foreign nations, rallies support for American policies abroad, and gathers information for use by policymakers in Washington.

Specialized bureaus in the department's Washington headquarters gather intelligence, cooperate with the Defense Department to coordinate military and foreign policy, represent the United States in international and scientific affairs, and deal with pressing global problems, such as the settlement of refugees, violations of human rights, and the international drug trade. Many people are not aware of the department's public services. Officials at consulates issue visas to foreign citizens trying to enter the United States. Consular officers stationed at home provide Americans with passports and help them find relatives who are missing overseas. In addition, the department's Bureau of Public Affairs publishes scores of useful information bulletins and important reference works on foreign policy.

The department and the Foreign Service are headed by the secretary of state, who is the senior member of the cabinet and the president's principal adviser on foreign affairs. The amount of authority a secretary wields varies greatly from administration to administration. Secretaries who have gotten along well with the president—such as George Marshall under Harry Truman and John Foster Dulles under Dwight D. Eisenhower—have exerted a great deal of influence on American foreign policy. Other secretaries—such as

President Richard Nixon (right) and his national security adviser Henry Kissinger (far left) toast the signing of the 1972 strategic arms treaty with the Soviet Union. Just beyond the glasses are Secretary of State William P. Rogers (left) and Communist Party General Secretary Leonid Brezhnev (right).

Robert Lansing under Woodrow Wilson and William P. Rogers under Richard M. Nixon—have been ignored in favor of other foreign affairs advisers.

In the past several decades, as American international responsibilities have increased, the Department of State has grown substantially. Between 1940 and 1980, its staff grew from 1,128 employees to 12,500, and the budget rose from $140 million to $2.3 billion. During the same period, however, the department's influence in the federal government waned. Whereas in its early years State was the only department with representatives abroad, today 45 different federal agencies have personnel stationed at American embassies and consulates. The National Security Council—a branch of the executive office created by the National Security Act of 1947—has competed with the State Department for the president's ear on foreign policy. During the 1950s, the department was severely weakened by the anticommunist campaign of Senator Joseph McCarthy, who claimed that a number of its officers were either Communists or Communist sympathizers. Recently, the department's effectiveness has been hampered by the growing number of terrorist attacks on its officials. In spite of all these handicaps, the department's consistently excellent leaders, along with its staff of professional diplomats, have enabled it to maintain its position as the preeminent force in the foreign affairs of the United States.

Benjamin Franklin, the most illustrious of several emissaries sent overseas by the colonial government during the revolutionary war, presents himself to the French court in 1778. As U.S. minister to France for nine years, Franklin secured valuable military aid.

TWO

Diplomacy and American Independence

The first four decades of the Department of State's history spanned an era when foreign relations were of decisive importance to the United States. In 1789, the year the department was founded, the United States was a fledgling nation with limited military power, a small population, and a weak central government. It was extremely vulnerable to attack by the European powers—Spain, England, and France—who coveted its vast lands and abundant natural resources. By 1823, however, the United States had secured its borders, doubled its territory, established an extensive foreign trade, and for the most part avoided conflicts with other nations. These achievements were due in large part to the efforts of the State Department. During these years, the department also helped develop two principles that would guide American policy for the rest of the 19th century: The United States should remain aloof from conflicts between European powers and avoid entangling itself in alliances; Europe should be discouraged from interfering in the Western Hemisphere.

The Department's Predecessor

The diplomatic history of the United States actually began several years before the formation of the State Department, during the revolutionary war, when the Continental Congress, the nation's first government, dispatched several emissaries to European capitals. The primary task of these first American diplomats was to persuade foreign leaders to assist the colonies in their attempt to achieve independence from Great Britain. Benjamin Franklin, the inventor, philosopher, and statesman from Pennsylvania, served as the first U.S. representative in Paris, where he purchased military supplies, secured a generous loan from the French government, and negotiated two treaties that proved vital to the colonial war effort. In one treaty, the French recognized America's right to nationhood, consented to establish normal trade relations, and agreed to exchange consular and diplomatic personnel; in the other, the countries formed a military alliance against a common enemy, Great Britain. (This was the only alliance the nation made with countries outside the Western Hemisphere until it joined the North Atlantic Treaty Organization in 1949.)

Unsatisfied with a strictly political role, Franklin took on several other functions as well, setting a precedent that future American diplomats would come to follow. Reporting on scientific developments in Europe, he became the nation's first science attaché (a diplomat with expertise in a particular area); attending art exhibits, salons, and concerts, he served as its first cultural attaché; and writing articles in favor of the American Revolution for French journals, he served as the first information officer. For these innovations and his remarkable facility for diplomacy, Franklin is often referred to as "the father of the American foreign service."

Other American agents received assignments in Spain, Prussia (a nation that later became part of Germany), Russia, Tuscany (a state that today composes the northwestern part of Italy), and the Netherlands and reported to the Continental Congress through the Committee on Foreign Affairs and its secretary, the noted pamphleteer Thomas Paine. They were generally less successful than Franklin. Some had difficulty convincing foreign leaders to meet with them, others had important documents pilfered by British agents, and one—Henry Laurens, the U.S. representative to the Netherlands—was captured by Great Britain on his way across the Atlantic and imprisoned in the Tower of London. As the number of American diplomats grew, the Committee on Foreign Affairs began to have trouble keeping track of reports coming in to its Philadelphia office from abroad. In 1779, the situation got worse when Paine was dismissed for publishing confidential government documents. With the

Committee on Foreign Affairs in a state of confusion, foreign envoys had little direction from the federal government and on many occasions made grave errors. For instance, a considerable scandal arose when Silas Deane, Franklin's fellow envoy in France, was accused of mismanaging French aid.

To improve matters, Congress finally decided in 1781 to establish a permanent executive department to manage foreign affairs. Thus was born the Department of Foreign Affairs (DFA), the predecessor of the Department of State. (Today, the Department of State calculates its age using the date on which the DFA was founded—January 10, 1781.) Robert R. Livingston, a delegate to Congress from New York who had helped draw up the Declaration of Independence, was named secretary of the new department and became the nation's first executive appointee. Livingston set up an office in Philadelphia with a staff of two under secretaries, a translator, and a clerk. He maintained an extensive correspondence with American diplomats and gave Congress regular reports on the state of relations with foreign nations. At the time, American diplomatic officials were of three types—ministers and consuls assigned to countries that had recognized the United States and unofficial agents in nations that had not yet done so. The diplomatic corps did not include ambassadors, because American leaders "regarded the title as pretentious and unsuited for a modest country, proud of its simple democratic ideals," in the words of one historian. Consequently, ministers ran the nation's foreign missions. Their work consisted primarily of diplomatic duties: negotiating treaties, representing the United States in the assigned country, and sending regular reports to the Department of Foreign Affairs on political, economic, and cultural matters. Consuls ran subordinate branches of missions, called consulates, and focused on providing assistance to Americans living in or visiting their districts. (It should be noted, however, that in some countries, consuls were the only U.S. representatives and in those places performed both diplomatic and consular tasks.)

The Treaty of Paris

During Livingston's tenure, a team of American diplomats opened talks with the British aimed at ending the revolutionary war. The four-man American peace commission consisted of Franklin (minister to France), Laurens (whom the British released from prison for the purpose of negotiating), John Adams (assistant minister to France), and John Jay (minister to Spain). Much to their consternation, the commissioners were initially put under the direction of the

American and British officials sign the 1783 Treaty of Paris, ending the revolutionary war. The pact was America's foremost diplomatic achievement during the eight-year history of the Department of Foreign Affairs, the State Department's predecessor.

French foreign minister, the Comte de Vergennes, in accordance with an agreement between Congress and the French government. But when they learned that Vergennes did not support their primary demand—British acknowledgment of American independence—and that his secretary had secretly encouraged the British to reject American demands for a piece of territory east of the Mississippi, the commissioners decided to sit down at the peace table without the French. Recognizing an opportunity to damage the alliance between France and the Americans, the British agreed to separate negotiations and proved quite amenable to American demands. Signed on September 3, 1783, the Treaty of Paris brought the revolutionary war to an official close (actual hostilities had ended in 1781), recognized the independence of the United States, and established the new nation's boundaries: the Mississippi River in the west, the northern border of Florida in the south, the Atlantic Ocean in the east, and the Great Lakes in the north. It also granted the United States fishing rights off the coast of Newfoundland (an island off the southeast ern coast of Canada then controlled by the British) in exchange for American promises to urge state governments to return property confiscated from colonists who remained loyal to the British during the revolutionary war.

In 1784, John Jay replaced Livingston as secretary of the Department of Foreign Affairs. Prior to becoming a diplomat, Jay had served as president of the Continental Congress and as the first chief justice of the state of New York. Secretary Jay concentrated on expanding foreign trade and securing recognition of the United States. Efforts in the former area were hampered by Spanish, British, and French dominance of markets in Europe and the Caribbean. As a result, American officials focused on tapping relatively undeveloped markets such as North Africa and the Far East. In 1787, Jay assigned consuls to the faraway cities of Tangier, Morocco, and Canton, China, to help American companies establish foreign outlets. Jay also tried to set up consulates in several other nations but Congress, which favored minimal spending for foreign affairs, blocked his efforts.

Overall, the Department of Foreign Affairs met with limited success during its nine-year history, in part because of congressional stinginess. Livingston and Jay were also hamstrung by small staffs, vague job descriptions, limited authority over American diplomats, and insufficient freedom to host foreign representatives. In addition, the department suffered from the absence of a

Before becoming the first chief justice of the United States, John Jay served as secretary of the Department of Foreign Affairs from 1784 to 1789. Under Jay's direction, the department helped expand American foreign trade by opening several new consulates overseas.

separate executive branch and the general impotence of the federal government under the Articles of Confederation, America's first constitution, in which the functions and limits of the government were defined.

The Creation of the Department of State

Eventually, the federal government's ineffectiveness in foreign policy, along with other shortcomings—its inability to ease economic depression and reconcile conflicts between the states—convinced American leaders to reexamine the Articles of Confederation. Between May and September 1787, the nation's most experienced and talented men convened in Philadelphia and hammered out a new governing document, the U.S. Constitution. The final version, ratified by the states between 1787 and 1789, for the first time gave the federal government the power to levy taxes and regulate interstate trade. It also significantly expanded federal power in the area of foreign affairs. Article II, the section of the document outlining presidential powers, empowered the chief executive to make treaties with foreign nations, to appoint ambassadors, and to receive foreign envoys. The Constitution also gave Congress a considerable role in making foreign policy. The Senate was given power to approve or reject treaties and ambassadorial appointments, and the entire legislature was given power to appropriate funds for foreign affairs. By dividing responsibility for foreign affairs between the legislative and executive branches, the Constitution ensured that neither would become too powerful. But by not identifying either as the final authority, it set the stage for endless conflict between the two branches.

Although the executive branch was checked by the legislature in creating foreign policy, the president had free reign in carrying out policy. To aid him in this task, on July 27, 1789, Congress voted to keep intact the Department of Foreign Affairs, which became the first executive agency of the new government. The Constitution had not specifically authorized the formation of this or any other department, but in stipulating that the president could "require the opinion, in writing, of the principal officer in each of the executive departments," it had acknowledged that departments would be created. The act officially establishing the department was vague about its role, saying that it should function "in such a manner as the president of the United States shall from time to time instruct." George Washington, the nation's first president, made it clear, as did many of his successors, that he regarded the department as an extension of presidential power in foreign affairs. He considered it a tool for seeking his own policy aims, rather than a truly independent force.

In 1789, after the federal government was reorganized under the Constitution, the Department of Foreign Affairs was renamed the Department of State and given a number of domestic tasks. Here, Thomas Jefferson (second from left), the first head of the new department, meets with President George Washington (seated) and other cabinet members.

Within two months, Congress had a change of heart about providing for a single department dedicated exclusively to foreign affairs. On September 15, 1789, the lawmakers changed the department's name to the Department of State and gave it several domestic duties. The department was assigned to keep official records, issue patents and copyrights, conduct the census, operate the nation's first mint, manage government printing, and run the mail service. It also became responsible for channeling messages back and forth between the federal government and various state governors. Under the act of September 15, the head of the department was designated the secretary of state. The secretary would later become an original member of the cabinet, a body of advisers to the president that, although never mentioned in a statute, became a recognized institution during the 1790s, evolving out of informal meetings of President Washington's staff.

The First Secretary of State

George Washington appointed Thomas Jefferson, the illustrious statesman who earlier had written the first draft of the Declaration of Independence and served as governor of Virginia, as the first secretary of state. At the time, Jefferson was stationed in Paris as the U.S. minister to France, and it took him until

March 1790 to wrap up unfinished business and return to the United States. In the interim, John Jay served as acting secretary of state. A man of keen intellect, diverse knowledge, and boundless energy, Jefferson had a lasting effect on the Department of State. First, he helped the president become dominant over Congress in foreign affairs, an arrangement that continued during several subsequent administrations. Giving the president primary responsiblity for foreign affairs, he argued, reduced the possibility of abrupt shifts in policy, enhanced the nation's ability to act decisively in times of crisis, and facilitated communication with other nations.

Jefferson also established an important principle regarding the recognition of new foreign governments. In the early 1790s, the French king was overthrown and replaced by a new government that in name was a republic but that in reality was a dictatorship of the radical Jacobin party under a middle-class

On July 14, 1789, a Parisian mob stormed the Bastille, a state prison, during a rebellion against the French king. After the French Revolution, President Washington considered cutting diplomatic ties with France, but Jefferson convinced him to ignore internal developments in other nations when deciding whether to maintain relations with them.

During his three-and-a-half year tenure as secretary of state, Thomas Jefferson set up the Diplomatic Service and the Consular Service (forerunners of the Foreign Service). Members of the Diplomatic Service handled political duties; consular officials assisted American citizens abroad.

lawyer named Maximilien Robespierre. When an envoy from the new revolutionary government traveled to the United States, Washington at first refused to receive him because of objections to the oppressive policies of Robespierre and his associates during the Reign of Terror. Eventually, however, Jefferson convinced Washington to change his mind, arguing that "every nation has the right to govern itself internally under what form it pleases." Jefferson's insistence on disregarding a nation's political structure when deciding whether to acknowledge that nation's government was subsequently adopted as general policy by George Washington and was maintained by all of his successors up to Woodrow Wilson, who became president in 1913.

During his five-year tenure, the nation's first secretary of state made two important institutional innovations. First, he formalized the existing distinction between consular and diplomatic personnel by creating a diplomatic service and a consular service and assigned all U.S. representatives abroad to one or the other. These divisions remained intact until 1924. Second, he began the practice of hiring talented officials from other government divisions on a temporary basis to conduct important overseas negotiations. The use of these

French captain Napoleon Bonaparte takes a British general captive during one of the several wars that the European powers fought between 1789 and 1815. Under the policy of neutrality instituted by Washington and Jefferson, the United States remained aloof from these conflicts.

so-called special agents helped the department operate with a relatively small number of permanent foreign representatives. Although it was the ranking executive agency in the U.S. government, State still possessed few resources. In 1790, there were only two foreign missions and five consulates; the budget for foreign operations, called the Foreign Fund, averaged only $40,000 a year. In the department's headquarters in Philadelphia, Jefferson employed a staff of two chief clerks, three other clerks, a part-time translator, and two custodians.

Jefferson's most important contribution was helping Washington develop an overall strategy for preserving the nation's security. At Jefferson's urging, Washington decided that the best way to cope with America's vulnerability to attack by the European powers was to adopt a policy of neutrality—of avoiding alliances, staying out of foreign disputes, and generally shunning most interactions with foreign governments. On April 22, 1793, the president issued the Neutrality Proclamation, much of which was written by Jefferson. The proclamation declared that the conduct of the United States should be "friendly and impartial toward the belligerent powers" and that American citizens found guilty of assisting the belligerents would be prosecuted. Congress made this policy a law in the Neutrality Act of 1794.

In Pursuit of Neutrality

In attempting to remain aloof from foreign entanglements, the United States was assisted by circumstances. Between 1789 (when the French Revolution began) and 1815 (when Napoleon Bonaparte, the French emperor, was defeated at Waterloo, abdicated, and was exiled) Britain, Spain, and France were almost continually at war with each other. These conflicts left the European powers with little energy for meddling in the affairs of the New World. With the danger of foreign intervention reduced, the United States was able to concentrate on developing its resources, building its economy, and securing its borders.

American leaders also took advantage of the European nations' preoccupation with continental wars to press territorial and other demands. During the course of the 1790s, conflicts developed with Great Britain over various issues. The British government had refused to surrender several North American forts that they had promised in the Treaty of Paris to relinquish. In addition, Britain had begun seizing American vessels on the high seas and forcing American sailors against their will to fight in the British navy against France. For their part, Americans refused to repay debts to British creditors incurred prior to the American Revolution. As tensions mounted, John Jay, who was then serving as the first chief justice of the United States, traveled as special agent to London to attempt to negotiate a solution. Anxious to avoid war with the United States because of other commitments in Europe, British leaders were in a conciliatory mood. On November 19, 1794, Jay signed a treaty with Great Britain under which the latter agreed to evacuate its frontier forts. Two other questions—the debt issue and a dispute over America's northern boundary with British territories in Canada—were referred to commissions composed of representatives of both sides. After its signing, Jay's Treaty, as it became known, raised a great deal of controversy in the United States because it left several issues unsettled. Nevertheless, it was finally approved by the Senate in 1796 and ultimately helped the United States avoid war with Britain for another 16 years.

After receiving word about the Jay Treaty, Spanish leaders feared that the United States intended to aid Great Britain in its European wars. In order to prevent an Anglo-American alliance, Spain, too, signed a treaty with the United States. Negotiated by Thomas Pinckney, a special agent, the pact granted the United States free navigation of the Mississippi River and expanded American holdings in the Spanish-controlled region of Florida. Spain also agreed to restrain Indians in Florida from crossing the border into the United States to conduct raids. By 1796, when Congress approved the Jay and Pinckney treaties, the United States had done much to free the country from foreign domination.

In his Farewell Address of 1796, President Washington reiterated the importance of his neutrality policy:

> The great rule of conduct for us in regard to foreign nations is. . . . to have with them as little political (as distinct from commercial) connection as possible. . . . Why, by interweaving our destiny with that of any part of Europe, entangle our peace and prosperity in the toils of European ambition, rivalship, interest, humor or caprice. . . . it is our true policy to steer clear of permanent alliances with any portion of the foreign world, so far, I mean, as we are now at liberty to do it.

Under the next president, John Adams, American neutrality was threatened by a conflict with France that arose from the French navy's repeated seizures of American vessels carrying nonmilitary goods to England. As relations with France became strained, the American people—most of whom had strong emotional ties to either England or France—encouraged their leaders to take sides. Complicating matters was the country's continuing official alliance with France. In 1800, Adams took decisive action to defuse the crisis, concluding the Treaty of Mortefontaine with France. The pact released the United States from its alliance with France on the condition that American businessmen drop their financial claims for the seizure of American vessels. Because these claims were worth almost $20 million, the treaty caused tremendous damage to Adams's party, the Federalists. But it left the nation completely free of alliances.

The Louisiana Purchase

The treaty of Mortefontaine seemed to engender an atmosphere of mutual trust betweeen France and the United States. But soon thereafter, Napoleon began to pursue plans to build an empire in North America. In 1802, France purchased from Spain the territory of Louisiana, a massive uncharted region west of the Mississippi River, full of wide plains, dense forests, and fertile soil.

Thomas Jefferson, who had taken over as president in 1801, saw Napoleon's design as a threat to the future of the United States. He dispatched James Monroe, the minister to England, and Robert Livingston, the minister to France, to Paris with orders to purchase the port of New Orleans, a small part of Louisiana. By the time negotiations began, however, Napoleon's fortunes had turned sour. A disastrous expedition by part of his army to put down a slave revolt on the Caribbean island of Haiti—during which thousands of French soldiers had caught yellow fever and died—convinced Napoleon to abandon his grandiose scheme to control North America.

Desperately needing funds for the treasury—and hoping to regain the Americans as allies—in 1803, Napoleon notified Monroe and Livingston that he was willing to sell Louisiana. Because of the primitive state of communications in those days, the American representatives did not have the option of consulting the president on the new offer. They decided to go ahead and accept it anyway—obtaining Louisiana for $11 milliion, only $1 million more than they had hoped to spend on the port of New Orleans.

The War of 1812

During Jefferson's second term as president, the recurring conflict between France and England intensified. Both combatants stepped up their campaigns against American shipping. The British went so far as to kidnap American sailors from waterfront locations and from merchant ships at sea. The British also stirred up resentment by refusing to withdraw from territories around the Great Lakes and by encouraging Indian attacks against American settlements. Amid this turmoil, American diplomats did a valiant job of keeping the country out of foreign disputes. Diplomatic solutions were proposed and economic measures tried. But by 1812 American shippers were cut off from Europe and American leaders could no longer resist pressure from the American people and hawks (those who favored war) in Congress to declare war on one or both of the belligerents. James Madison, the president at the time, finally chose to engage Great Britain rather than France because the British, with greater sea power, had done more damage to American shipping. And so began the War of 1812.

Members of the diplomatic service helped resolve the crisis. Negotiations began in London only a week after the declaration of war on June 18, 1812. But for more than two years, American representatives—who included John Quincy Adams and Henry Clay—were unable to persuade the British to accept their demands. Finally, they were forced to accept an agreement that ended

A 19th-century etching called The Peace of Ghent *celebrates the treaty that ended the War of 1812. State Department negotiators are depicted as Romans in a triumphal parade. The treaty was merely an armistice, but it was considered an American victory because it meant the United States had fought a superior foe to a standstill.*

the fighting but did not address the problems that had given rise to the war. The Treaty of Ghent was signed on December 24, 1814. (Because communications traveled slowly in those days, the war continued for another two weeks and concluded with the dramatic Battle of New Orleans in which Andrew Jackson, who later became the seventh U.S. president, first gained national attention.)

John Quincy Adams

In 1817 James Monroe became president and named John Quincy Adams as his secretary of state. Adams had previously held several posts in the diplomatic service. At the precocious age of 14 he had gone to St. Petersburg as a private secretary to the American minister to Russia. In his mid-twenties he had been named minister resident to the Netherlands. Later he had served as minister to Russia and minister to Great Britain. Indeed, in an age when most American representatives abroad regarded their assignments as temporary breaks from their careers in domestic politics, Adams was the closest thing to a career foreign service officer. Surprisingly enough, his personality was hardly that of a typical diplomat. According to one historian, "his manners were stiff and disagreeable; he told the truth bluntly . . . and never took pain to conciliate anyone." But Adams more than made up for his curtness with keen intelligence, remarkable industry, and a gift for languages.

Upon taking office, Adams found the State Department in disarray. Bills had been left unpaid. Records were poorly kept. There was no clear chain of command. To eliminate the backlog of paperwork, Adams and his staff often had to work seven days a week during his first months in office. Finally, in 1818, Adams made the first serious attempt to organize the department. He instituted a new accounting system, developed new operating procedures, clarified job descriptions, and enforced greater discipline.

In addition to improving the administrative efficiency of the department, Adams played a leading role in deliberations with foreign nations. In 1818, he concluded an agreement with Britain under which the British and American military forces along the Canadian border were reduced. The following year, he negotiated a treaty with Spain that clarified the American border with Mexico and for the first time recognized that American claims stretched to the Pacific Ocean. Perhaps Adams's most significant diplomatic achievement was the settlement of a dispute with Spain over territory in Florida.

The dispute began when General Andrew Jackson and his army of 2,000 men invaded Florida on a punitive operation against the Seminole Indians. Because he had difficulty tracking down the Indians, who took refuge in the swamps, Jackson decided instead to seize several Spanish forts, from which the Seminoles had often received food, ammunition, and encouragement for their raids on American frontier settlements. By May 1818, Jackson had seized every important post in Florida and deposed the Spanish governor. Rather than meekly acceding to the capture of its territory, the Spanish government registered strong protests. At first, President Monroe repudiated his aggressive general's campaign and restored Florida to Spain. But through shrewd negotiating tactics, Secretary Adams reacquired the territory. Under the Adams-Onaís Treaty, signed on February 22, 1819, the United States obtained Florida, all other Spanish lands east of the Mississippi, and the European power's claims in Oregon in exchange for $5 million.

Adams also played a major role in formulating one of the guiding principles of American foreign policy, the Monroe Doctrine. Set forth by President James Monroe in his 1823 message to Congress, the doctrine in essence declared

Before being appointed secretary of state in 1817, John Quincy Adams held a number of diplomatic posts. As secretary, Adams improved the organization of the State Department, negotiated several major treaties, and helped formulate the Monroe Doctrine.

that "the Western Hemisphere belongs to the United States." It demanded an end to European colonization of and interference in the New World and warned that any further attempt by a European nation to gain control of American territory or the violation of the sovereignty of an existing nation would be regarded as an act of aggression. At the same time, it restated Washington's Neutrality Proclamation, stating "in the wars of the European powers in matters relating to themselves we have never taken part, nor does it comport with our policy to do so."

The doctrine emerged principally from the desire to secure two regions of the Western Hemisphere—the Pacific Northwest and Latin America. In Adams's view, the Pacific Northwest was threatened by the growing Russian fur trade, and Latin America faced the possibility of intervention by France to help Spain regain colonies that had won independence. British officials were equally concerned about these developments and expressed an interest in making a joint declaration, but Adams convinced Monroe to make his independent statement to Congress. At first, the United States lacked sufficient resources to enforce the doctrine and it was, in fact, the naval power of its new ally, Great Britain, that kept other European powers out of the Western Hemisphere. However, in the late 19th and early 20th centuries, as the United States itself became a military power, it frequently invoked the doctrine to justify intervention in Latin America. Even today, the doctrine has influenced the actions of some American policymakers.

For most of the 19th century—after Andrew Jackson led American forces to victory at the Battle of New Orleans (pictured here)—the United States steered clear of foreign entanglements. During this period, the reputation of the State Department waned, especially after Jackson, upon becoming president, began filling its ranks with political appointees.

THREE

The Age of Free Security

In 1815, the Napoleonic wars came to an end, ushering in a long period of relative peace in Europe. Stability on the eastern side of the Atlantic enabled the United States to pursue a policy of neutrality for the rest of the 19th century and to devote most of its attention to westward expansion and industrial growth. During this period, the Department of State—with few foreign disputes to settle and no alliances to maintain—dwindled in importance. Its budget remained limited, its ranks were dominated by apathetic political appointees, and its supposed status as the senior executive department was generally ignored. Not surprisingly, public regard for diplomats declined. The American people's low regard for overseas emissaries was perhaps best described by Congressman Benjamin Stanton of Ohio, who said in 1859 that he knew of "no area of the public service that is more emphatically useless than the diplomatic service—none in the world."

Growth, Organization, and the Spoils System

In spite of the department's low status, it did enlarge its network of foreign representatives and became increasingly organized during the 19th century. Between 1830 and 1860, the number of American diplomatic missions grew from 15 to 33 and the number of consulates increased from 83 to 282. Most of these posts were located in Europe and Latin America, but a few were in more remote places such as China, Japan, and Hawaii. In 1825, when John Quincy Adams became president, his successor as secretary of state, Henry Clay, resumed Adams's effort to make the department more efficient. Clay sent Congress a report on the department's organization in which he pointed out that of the 15 categories of work performed by his staff, only 8 involved foreign affairs; the other 7, he argued, should be assigned to a separate—as yet nonexistent—"home" department. Congress turned down Clay's request but six years later approved major changes made by his successor, Louis McLane.

As secretary of state under President Andrew Jackson, McLane organized the department's central office into seven bureaus—two to handle overseas correspondence (the Diplomatic and Consular Bureaus); three to take care of domestic duties (the Home Bureau, the Bureau of Pardons, Remissions, Copyrights, and Library, and the Bureau of Archives, Laws, and Commissions); and two to perform administrative tasks (the Disbursing Bureau and the Translating and Miscellaneous Bureau). To relieve his own administrative burden, McLane created the position of chief clerk and transferred to it responsibility for managing the day-to-day activities of the department. McLane's reorganization "proved particularly valuable," in the words of one historian, "because it established clear lines of responsibility and specific duties for individuals, while allowing for flexibility to meet future changes."

But at the same time that McLane improved the department's administration, the president introduced a practice that severely weakened the overseas staff. President Jackson began awarding most diplomatic and consular appointments to members of his party who had provided valuable support during his election campaign. Maintained for much of the 19th century, this practice—known as the spoils system—filled the ranks of the diplomatic and consular services with hundreds of men who had no previous experience and little interest in foreign affairs. They often could not even be counted upon to be familiar with basic diplomatic protocol (rules establishing the proper etiquette for diplomatic exchange). For example, John Randolph, minister to Russia under Jackson, upon first meeting the czar at his St. Petersburg palace, greeted him not with the traditional formal pleasantries but with the crudely informal question, "How'ya emperor? And how's the Madam?" To make matters worse, neither the diplomatic nor the consular service had any system for promotion or a training period for new members. Not surprisingly, few persons interested in a long career in government looked to the foreign service for employment.

A Few Diplomatic Accomplishments

In spite of the overall mediocrity of the American foreign service during the 19th century, on a few occasions American diplomats scored major victories. During the Mexican-American War (1846–48), President James Polk assigned Nicholas P. Trist, chief clerk in the State Department, to accompany an American force invading Mexico "to take advantage of circumstances, as they might arise, to negotiate peace." Led by General Winfield Scott, the force landed at the eastern port of Vera Cruz in March 1847 and by September 1848 had captured Mexico City and forced the government to surrender. Trist began peace negotiations with instructions from Polk to offer the termination of all claims by American citizens against the Mexican government in exchange for recognition of the Rio Grande as the Mexican-American border; $5 million for the part of New Mexico still controlled by Mexico; and up to $25 million for

Mexican troops overrun an American stronghold during the Mexican-American War (1846–48). After the United States won the war, the State Department's chief clerk, Nicholas Trist, negotiated a peace settlement in which Mexico ceded California to the United States.

the state of California. In November 1847, after negotiations were delayed several times, an impatient Polk ordered his envoy to return to the United States. But sensing that he was on the verge of a breakthrough, Trist remained in Mexico. On February 2, 1848, he signed the Treaty of Guadalupe Hidalgo, under which the United States obtained California, New Mexico, and the Rio Grande boundary for $15 million. Although the treaty was clearly a coup for the Americans, upon his return Trist was denounced by Polk as "an impudent scoundrel" for disobeying orders and was dismissed from his job. Eventually, however, Polk submitted the treaty to the Senate and it was approved.

William Seward, secretary of state under Presidents Abraham Lincoln and Andrew Johnson, brought the Department of State temporary prominence. During the Civil War, Seward and his staff at home and abroad enjoyed unqualified success in carrying out their principal task—convincing Great Britain not to provide financial or military support to the Confederate States. After the war, Seward defended the Monroe Doctrine against violation by the French, who had set up a puppet government in Mexico led by the Austrian

William Seward, secretary of state under Presidents Abraham Lincoln and Andrew Johnson, is best known for his purchase of Alaska from Russia—a deal then known as "Seward's Folly" because of the area's seeming uselessness.

archduke Maximilian. In 1866, Seward demanded the withdrawal of the French from the Western Hemisphere and convinced President Johnson to send 50,000 troops to the Mexican border to back up the demand. These actions proved pivotal in enabling Mexico eventually to expel French forces.

In 1867, Seward arranged with Russia for the purchase of Alaska for $7,200,000. Initially, many congressmen expressed skepticism about the deal, referring to it as "Seward's Folly." But after a number of them were given bribes by the Russian minister in Washington, the purchase was approved. In time, the land many of the American people then referred to as "Seward's ice box" turned out to possess strategic value and important natural resources.

Further Reorganization

In 1850, the Department of the Interior took over two of the State Department's domestic tasks—granting patents and taking the census. Later in the decade, the remainder of the State Department's domestic functions were transferred to other agencies. An act entitled "To Remodel the Diplomatic and Consular Systems of the United States," signed by President Franklin Pierce in 1856, called for further reorganization. The law significantly increased salaries for diplomatic representatives. It also instituted reforms in the consular corps. For many years, the only money consuls received was a percentage of the fees they charged for services. Fees ranged widely from consulate to consulate and often were exorbitant. The 1856 law established fixed fees that consuls had to charge for their services and required that these rates be posted prominently in each consulate. The bill also provided for consuls at larger missions to receive regular salaries.

The Least Active Period

Historians have judged the 30 years after the Civil War to be the least active in the entire history of American foreign relations. An absence of threats from abroad—a condition termed by some scholars "free security"—enabled Americans to concentrate on industrialization, urbanization, and the completion of westward expansion. One index of the low priority of foreign relations after the Civil War was the State Department's budget. Between 1860 and 1890, while the budget of some agencies more than doubled, State Department expenditures rose less than 40 percent. Although still nominally the senior cabinet officer, the secretary of state in many an administration received less attention from the White House than the secretary of treasury or secretary of war.

The spoils system continued to cause problems for the department. Every time a new president took office, the entire leadership of the home office and the consular and diplomatic services was overhauled. Cronyism was carried to extreme lengths in 1869, when President Ulysses S. Grant, prior to appointing his friend Elihu Washburne minister to France, made Washburne secretary of state for 12 days so that he could claim the honor of having held the office. Eventually, with every other government department similarly debilitated by the spoils system, a movement for reform took hold. The Civil Service League, founded in 1881, proposed legislation that would establish a civil service—a pool of career government workers—and require the majority of government positions to be filled by members of the service. In 1883, such a bill, the Pendleton Act, was passed. Ironically, it exacerbated the situation for the diplomatic and consular services. Because the bill did not apply to those divisions, they had to absorb most of the political appointees who previously would have been assigned to other departments.

The post–Civil War period also saw further reorganization of the Department of State. In 1870, Congress had reduced the Department of State's team of clerks from 48 to 31. To enable the department to function with a pared-down staff, Hamilton Fish, Grant's secretary of state, modified the bureau system. He divided the Diplomatic Bureau into two bureaus, each of which had responsibility for a specific geographical area; he did the same thing for the Consular Bureau. The First Diplomatic Bureau and the First Consular Bureau serviced Europe, China, and Japan, while the other pair of bureaus dealt with the rest of the world—Latin America, the Mediterranean region, Russia, Hawaii, and Liberia. In addition to setting up these four geographical bureaus, Fish consolidated all administrative tasks into two more bureaus—the Bureau of Indexes and Archives and the Bureau of Accounts.

Abandoning Isolationism

During the 1880s and 1890s, the American people began to take an increasing interest in foreign affairs. A series of economic depressions prompted many to support the expansion of foreign trade as a way of reducing surpluses of manufactured goods. Watching the European powers and Japan expand their colonial empires to include lands in Africa, the Middle East, and Asia, a number of prominent Americans encouraged their nation to acquire its own overseas territories. Supporters of expansionism, who included President Theodore Roosevelt and Senator Henry Cabot Lodge, thought that if the United States did not enter, even belatedly, into the scramble for colonies, they might never

Hamilton Fish, secretary of state under President Ulysses S. Grant, was one of several 19th-century secretaries of state who reorganized the State Department. In 1870, Fish set up the department's four geographic bureaus.

be able to protect their interests and markets. Many believed that the country should use a strengthened navy to enlarge and guarantee its share of foreign trade—an approach referred to as mercantile imperialism.

James G. Blaine, appointed secretary of state in 1889, was the first secretary to champion expansionist views in the State Department. Blaine sought to establish American bases in Haiti and Santo Domingo and negotiated an agreement with Great Britain and Germany that gave the United States joint control of the islands of Samoa. Blaine, an ardent advocate of the Monroe Doctrine, also attempted to increase the United States's involvement in Latin American affairs. He helped initiate construction of the Panama Canal, promoted trade with neighboring countries, and in 1889 organized the First Pan-American Conference, a meeting of Latin American and Caribbean leaders aimed at strengthening economic and political ties among the American republics. Delegates gathered in Washington after being treated to a 6,000-

mile tour of the United States. But when they finally sat down at the negotiating table and heard Blaine's plans for a Pan-American movement—a loose alliance of Western Hemisphere nations based on trade agreements and strategic alliances—they were unable to reach an accord. In the end, the only substantive action taken was the establishment of an office for the exchange of information about political and economic developments in the Americas. It was not until 50 years later that Blaine's proposals for hemispheric unity gained significant support.

During the early 1890s, a series of conflicts with foreign nations unleashed a new martial spirit in the United States. In March 1891, after 11 men of Italian descent were charged with murder in New Orleans, several newspapers called for war with Italy. In October of the same year, the United States came close to fighting a war with Chile after two American sailors on leave in the Chilean port of Valparaiso were killed by a mob of locals. In 1895, when Great Britain became embroiled in a border dispute with Venezuela, President Grover Cleveland forced the British to make concessions by invoking the Monroe Doctrine and threatening military action. During this last conflict, Theodore Roosevelt, then a member of the U.S. Civil Service Commission, said: "Let the fight come if it must. I rather hope that it will come soon. The clamor of the peace faction has convinced me that this country needs a war."

During the second half of the decade, proponents of war focused their attention on Cuba, where the Spanish colonial government had instituted harsh economic policies and killed thousands in a brutal resettlement program. Seeing a chance both to help a struggling neighbor and to open new markets for American goods, expansionists urged the American government to intervene on behalf of rebels who had begun a revolt against the Spanish in 1895. Jingoist editors, including William Randolph Hearst and Joseph Pulitzer, stirred up popular support for the Cuban rebels by publishing exaggerated accounts of Spanish atrocities. Finally, as a show of support, the United States sent the battleship *Maine* on a goodwill visit to Havana harbor, where it mysteriously blew up. After investigating the incident, Congress decided to declare war in April 1898.

The Spanish-American War, as it was known, took place in two hemispheres. In the east, an American naval group, led by Admiral William Dewey, acted with lightning speed, sailing from Hong Kong to the Spanish colony of the Philippines during the first week of the war. On May 1, Dewey defeated the Spanish fleet in a decisive battle in Manila Bay. A month later, the remainder of the Spanish navy was destroyed while attempting to penetrate a blockade the United States had imposed on Cuba. Finally, on July 17, after fierce fighting

The charred hull of the USS Maine *lies partially submerged in Cuba's Havana harbor after mysteriously blowing up in February 1898. In response to the sinking of the battleship, the United States declared war on Spain, Cuba's colonial ruler.*

in the Cuban mountains, American forces captured the island's capital, Santiago, and forced the Spanish to surrender.

The 10-week conflict, which Secretary of State John Hay dubbed the "splendid little war," was a major turning point for American power, markedly increasing the nation's standing in world affairs. Under the peace treaty, signed in Paris on December 10, 1898, the United States acquired a sizable colonial empire, receiving Puerto Rico and Guam outright, taking over Cuba as a protectorate, and purchasing the Philippines for $20 million. The conflict was also a major symbolic watershed. For the 122-year-old nation, it represented a complete break with the old tradition of isolationism, abstention, and withdrawal. No longer would the nation turn its back on international affairs. And no longer would the Department of State be considered a superfluous agency.

British leaders welcome a shipment of American aid provided under the Marshall Plan. The plan, an enormous program of American economic aid to rebuild the war-devastated economies of Western Europe, established the European Recovery Program and is considered today as one of the most effective counterattacks on poverty, desperation, and destruction in history.

FOUR

From World Power to Superpower

In the 16 years between the Spanish-American War (1898) and World War I (1914–18), the United States markedly expanded its international role. During that short period, the nation established itself as the dominant force in the Western Hemisphere. On numerous occasions, it intervened militarily and politically in Latin American countries to safeguard commercial interests or to install new leaders. In the process, American leaders revised the Monroe Doctrine. In its original form, the doctrine had warned the European powers not to colonize the Western Hemisphere any further, but it had not described America's own role in the region. In 1904, Theodore Roosevelt addressed this question, issuing the Roosevelt corollary to the Monroe Doctrine. He asserted that the United States was justified in imposing its will on Latin American countries where there was "chronic wrongdoing, or an impotence which results in a general loosening of the ties of civilized society."

Meanwhile, the United States used its colony in the Philippines as a base from which to expand its influence throughout the Far East, especially in China. John Hay, who served as secretary of state from 1898 to 1905, played a major role in developing America's China policy. Earlier in the 19th century, Chinese leaders, weakened by defeat in the Opium Wars (wars with Britain sparked by

President Theodore Roosevelt issued the Roosevelt corollary to the Monroe Doctrine, insisting that the United States had the right to intervene in weak or corrupt Latin American nations.

China's ban on the importation of opium), granted the United States trading rights in their country—along with Great Britain, France, Germany, Italy, and Russia. But by the late 1890s, Hay feared that the other imperialist powers were encroaching upon America's share of trade. In 1899, Hay sent a letter to the other powers asking them to agree with three principles: that no power should interfere with the trading rights of another nation within its sphere of influence; that Chinese tariff duties should be collected on all merchandise by Chinese officials; and that no power should levy discriminating harbor dues or railroad charges against other nations within its sphere. The next year he sent a second note, this time urging fellow powers to respect the territorial and administrative integrity of China. Accepted by the other nations until the 1930s, Hay's plan became known as the Open Door policy.

Growth and Reform

As the nation's spheres of influence grew, the Department of State's responsibilities increased. To help American businesses find new markets for their goods and to provide services to the rising number of Americans traveling or living abroad, scores of new consulates were set up overseas. To expand the nation's network of friends and allies abroad, several additional ambassadorships were created. Realizing the new importance of diplomacy, a group of businessmen, civil service reformers, congressmen, and State Department officials joined forces to improve the foreign service and the State Department. Their first aim was to eliminate the spoils system from the consular service. In 1905, Theodore Roosevelt, with the encouragement of his secretary of state, Elihu Root, issued an executive order requiring that appointments to all major consular offices be made on the basis of merit. A year later, Roosevelt signed a second executive order that instituted an examination to measure the relative merit of prospective appointees. State Department officials developed the test, which included both written and oral sections. Soon thereafter, Congress reformed the system for paying consuls. In the past, only a few consuls had received salaries and the rest were given a percentage of the fees they charged for services. Under the new system, all consuls were given salaries. All fees had to be passed on to the Department of the Treasury and an inspection board was set up to enforce this regulation.

Between 1900 and 1910, the number of employees in the State Department's home office increased from 40 to 210. In that period, Congress raised the department's budget from $3.4 million to $44.9 million. Under Secretary Root, the department added, on an experimental basis, an additional regional bureau in the home office to keep track of U.S. representatives in a specific region. The new bureau had a much narrower focus than the regional bureaus set up by Secretary Hamilton Fish in the 1870s. Called the Bureau of Far Eastern Affairs, it was assigned to monitor economic and political developments in that region and to prepare policy papers for the department's leadership. In 1909, Secretary of State Philander C. Knox set up three more regional bureaus—for Western Europe, the Near East, and Latin America. Several consuls and secretaries were recalled from abroad to staff these bureaus and to provide their firsthand expertise. Knox also established a Division of Information to provide American diplomats around the world with news about international events involving the United States. Later in 1909, President William Howard Taft reformed the diplomatic service along the same lines on which Roosevelt had modified the consular service in 1905 and 1906. Appointment regulations were revamped to emphasize merit, and oral and written exams were instituted to test prospective diplomatic appointees. In 1911, for the first time, Congress disbursed funds for the purchase, construction, and repair of embassy buildings.

World War I

In the summer of 1914, war broke out across Europe after a Serbian nationalist's assassination of the Austrian archduke Franz Ferdinand upset the continent's precarious balance of power. With the outbreak of hostilities, the State Department's workload jumped dramatically—even before the United States became a combatant. During the three years that America remained neutral, its diplomats helped President Woodrow Wilson defend the nation's right to trade and use the oceans freely. When those rights were violated—for example, when German submarines sank American passenger vessels bound for Britain—U.S. representatives abroad registered protests and sought restitution. Consuls stationed in Europe assisted American companies in becoming the principal suppliers of armaments and foodstuffs to the Allies and offered aid to American citizens whose lives or property were threatened by the fighting. State Department officials were also responsible for approving loans provided to the Allies by American financiers. At home, the State Department's headquarters added more than 150 permanent employees and 400 temporary workers.

The war exposed a major problem in the foreign service: The appointment of foreign envoys to specific posts rather than to ranks in the service made it difficult to shift staff between embassies. This defect became apparent when several American missions had to be closed because the United States had broken off relations with the host nation or because hostilities had threatened the security of foreign representatives. Officials were reluctant to shift the affected envoys to other missions without legal guidelines for doing so. In 1915, Congress eliminated the confusion by passing a bill that required diplomats to be appointed to levels in the service rather than to specific positions.

Under President Wilson, there were two secretaries of state. The first, William Jennings Bryan, took office in 1913; one of the best known men in America, he had delivered a landmark speech against the gold standard in 1896 and had run unsuccessfully for president several times on an anti-imperialist campaign. Secretary Bryan assumed an unusually active role in domestic policy, on several occasions serving as a mediator between the president and agricultural interests who sought reforms of the banking system. He also worked closely with Wilson to develop a foreign policy based on moral principle. As they interpreted it, moral principle meant seeking peace through several means—making diplomatic initiatives, promoting adherence to international law, and convincing undeveloped countries to set up governments based on democratic constitutions. At times, Bryan's attitudes put him at odds with career members of the State Department, who in his mind were not sufficiently idealistic.

After World War I began, the department's leadership struggled. In 1915 Bryan resigned because of disagreements with Wilson over how best to preserve the nation's neutrality. The secretary thought that Wilson's reprimand of the German government for the sinking of a British passenger vessel, the *Lusitania*, was unduly provocative. He also thought that Wilson's insistence on

The British passenger ship Lusitania *sails out of New York harbor on its last voyage. On May 7, 1915, the ship, with 127 Americans aboard, sank after it was torpedoed by a German submarine. The United States exerted intense pressure on Germany, demanding that it issue an apology and pay reparations.*

sending additional passenger vessels overseas after several had been torpedoed was "a sort of moral treason." Bryan was replaced by New York lawyer Robert Lansing, who at first played a valuable part in winning reparations from Germany. In 1916, he convinced German leaders to apologize and provide an indemnity for the *Lusitania* incident. But after the United States entered the war in April 1917, Lansing had little influence. Instead Wilson turned for advice on foreign affairs to his friend Edward M. House, a businessman and former colonel in the Texas militia. House's office in New York became known as the "Little State Department."

After the war ended, Lansing was named a member of the American delegation to the peace talks in Paris. But Wilson did most of the negotiating himself and, once the pact was concluded, refused to heed Lansing's advice to compromise with those in the Senate who opposed, and ultimately defeated, the treaty, known as the Treaty of Versailles. When Wilson suffered a debilitating stroke in 1919, Lansing took advantage of the situation to become temporary head of the cabinet. But when the president recovered somewhat, he lambasted Lansing for unconstitutionally exercising presidential power and forced him to resign.

Return to Isolationism

After the Senate rejected the Treaty of Versailles in 1919, the United States for years resisted accepting international responsibilities that matched its actual power. The reputation of the State Department again slipped. The sole exceptions to this trend in the 1920s were the Washington Naval Disarmament Conference of 1921–22, hosted by Secretary of State Charles Evans Hughes, and the Paris Peace Pact of 1928, spearheaded by Secretary of State Frank Kellogg. Eventually ratified by 62 nations, the pact won a Nobel Peace Prize for Secretary Kellogg. But, like the naval conference of 1921–22, the pact provided for no means of enforcement and proved ineffective against the surge of aggression by Germany and Japan in the next decade.

The Creation of the Foreign Service

The movement that began in the late 1800s to improve the foreign service culminated in 1924 with the Rogers Act, the most significant piece of foreign service legislation ever passed by Congress. Written primarily by State Department officials and sponsored in Congress by Congressman John Jacob

Frank Kellogg (seated, center), President Calvin Coolidge's secretary of state, poses with diplomats from Chile and Peru. For his resolution of a border conflict between those two nations and his sponsorship of a treaty under which 62 nations renounced war, Kellogg won the 1929 Nobel Peace Prize.

Rogers of Massachusetts, the bill merged the consular and diplomatic services in a single organization called The Foreign Service of the United States. Most foreign representatives had by then become, as a result of Taft's and Roosevelt's reforms, career officers rather than temporary envoys. Hence, the new Foreign Service became the overseas equivalent of the Civil Service, an organization of skilled professionals who filled all positions in embassies and consulates—except for ambassadorships, ministerial positions, and relatively menial jobs that were filled by local laborers. The new service, which like its predecessors was an arm of the State Department, consisted of 633 officers, 511 in the consular service and 122 in the diplomatic service.

New members of the service were initially to be assigned to either the diplomatic or consular branch, but most would eventually serve in both, under a regular system of rotation established by the Rogers Act. All members of the service were to receive retirement and disability benefits and frequent home leave at the expense of the government. The act also significantly raised salaries, which meant that no longer did most foreign representatives have to be independently wealthy. This ended upper-class domination of the diplomatic corps. The act's reforms suddenly made foreign service an attractive career to many. The year before the act was passed, only 13 people applied for foreign service positions, but the year after, 172 applications were received.

Secretary Cordell Hull

The tenure of Cordell Hull as Secretary of State (1933–44) was the longest in American history. A courtly, soft-spoken Tennessean, the former senator never achieved a close relationship with President Franklin Roosevelt; like

Cordell Hull, President Franklin D. Roosevelt's secretary of state, won the 1945 Nobel Peace Prize for helping to establish the United Nations. Hull's 12-year tenure was the longest of any secretary of state.

numerous successors, Roosevelt chose to be, in many regards, his own secretary of state. Nevertheless, Hull's preparatory work for the founding of the United Nations won him a Nobel Peace Prize in 1945. Less noted by historians but also of significance was Hull's work on the reciprocal Trade Agreements Act of 1934.

This major law was intended to cut the tariffs, or duties, on foreign imports, especially the Hawley-Smoot Tariff of 1930, widely blamed for bringing on the Great Depression. The 1934 act empowered the president to lower existing rates up to 50 percent for those nations willing to make reciprocal concessions. By 1947 Hull and his successors had negotiated agreements with 29 nations, thus cutting duties on 70 percent of America's imports. World War II, like World War I, increased the responsibilities of both the department and the Foreign Service. During the conflict, State Department officials helped evacuate Americans from combat zones, provided assistance to refugees, and negotiated prisoner-of-war exchanges, among other functions. But several important foreign affairs activities were assigned to new temporary agencies: the Board of Economic Warfare, the Office of War Information, and the Office of Strategic Services.

Postwar Expansion

After the war, the Department of State helped the nation assume a prominent role in rebuilding Europe and reshaping the international political order. To enable the department to cope with its expanded duties, Secretary of State James F. Byrnes, a former senator and Supreme Court justice, gathered several temporary wartime organizations—including the Office of War Information and the Board for Economic Warfare—into the permanent structure of the department. During the last year of the war, Byrnes's predecessor, Edward R. Stettinius, Jr., had created new bureaus to deal with trade relations, cultural diplomacy, public information, and interactions with federal agencies that gathered intelligence.

In 1946 Congress upgraded the Foreign Service. The Foreign Service Act gave the organization its own head, called the director general; established the Foreign Service Institute to offer advanced training for Foreign Service officers; and created the Foreign Service Reserve, a pool of professionals in such fields as law, medicine, and economics. The bill also improved assignment policy, promotion procedures, allowances and benefits, home leave, and the retirement system.

Containment Policy

By 1947 the alliance the United States had cultivated with the Soviet Union during World War II had broken down. In violation of agreements made during the war, the Soviet Union had consolidated political control over the Eastern European countries that Red Army troops had occupied during the fighting. Stalin had promised Roosevelt at the Yalta Conference of February 1945 that he would hold free elections in these nations, but after the war governments loyal to Moscow were forcefully established in Poland, Czechoslovakia, Hungary, Romania, Bulgaria, Albania, East Germany, and Yugoslavia.

Policymakers groped for ways to deal with the Soviet threat. In 1947, one of the State Department's leading authorities on the Soviet Union, George F. Kennan, published an article in which he proposed a new strategy. He wrote that "the main element of any United States policy toward the Soviet Union must be that of a long-term, patient but firm and vigilant containment of Russian expansive tendencies." This basic idea, containment, quickly became the foundation of American policy *vis-à-vis* the Soviets. From 1947 to 1950, it would inform several important foreign policy programs undertaken by the nation and the State Department.

The first program was initiated in March 1947, when Greece and Turkey faced subversion from Soviet-backed insurgents. President Truman persuaded Congress to appropriate $400 million in emergency assistance to each nation, arguing that in order to prevent the fall of free nations, it was necessary to attack the conditions of "misery and want" that make communism attractive. This attempt to forestall the spread of communism by providing economic aid became known as the Truman Doctrine.

The Marshall Plan

Within three months this concept was extended to Western Europe. What came to be known as the Marshall Plan was largely the handiwork of Department of State employees—career people and political appointees—but it gained its first impetus from a soldier. Throughout World War II George C. Marshall held the position of army chief of staff. Although credited by many of his contemporaries and, later, by historians as the architect of victory in that conflict, he was so self-effacing that he refused to be decorated while young men were dying abroad. As secretary of state from 1947 to 1949, he was so unpretentious that he refused a bodyguard, saying that he would "rather be murdered than embarrassed."

The Marshall Plan was announced in a typically low-key speech at the Harvard University commencement ceremonies on June 5, 1947. Marshall described the disintegrating economy of Europe in the wake of World War II. He said:

> It is logical that the United States should do whatever it is able to assist in the return of normal economic health to the world, without which there can be no political stability and no assured peace. Our policy is directed not against any country or doctrine but against hunger, poverty, desperation and chaos.

He emphasized that the initiative for recovery had to come from the European nations themselves, which would be expected to join in a cooperative effort to put the entire continent back on its feet.

The Marshall Plan marked a dramatic departure from the isolationism that the United States had embraced after World War I. To convince the country at large, the Truman administration launched a massive public relations campaign. Describing the growing desperation abroad, Harry Truman urged every citizen to institute meatless Tuesdays and to reduce consumption of poultry and eggs. Children promised to clean their plates; bakeries reported measures to reduce waste. The Democratic administration, keenly aware that the opposition party had won the off-year election in 1946, reached out to have twice-weekly meetings with the Republican chairman of the Senate Foreign Relations Committee, Senator Arthur H. Vandenberg of Michigan, a former isolationist. A Select Committee on Foreign Aid, chaired by Congressman Christian Herter, was organized with a geographical and political cross section of the House membership. Deployed in five subcommittees—each focused on a different area of Europe—the Herter committee further softened conservative opposition. The European Recovery Program passed the Senate on March 13, 1948, by a vote of 69 to 17, followed by a favorable House vote on March 31 of 329 to 74.

The Marshall Plan legislation provided for an Economic Cooperation Administration (ECA) to administer the aid program in Europe. The ECA was expected to consult with the State Department but was responsible only to the president. Over the 4-year period during which the Marshall Plan was formally in operation, Congress appropriated $13.3 billion for European recovery—equivalent to more than $100 billion in 1987 dollars.

By the end of 1951, the European gross national product (the total value of a nation or area's annual output of goods and services) grew 33.5 percent. In the 35 years that followed, the per capita standard of living of the 16

George Marshall was appointed secretary of state in 1947 after serving as U.S. army chief of staff during World War II. Under Marshall's program for European recovery, the United States provided more than $13.3 billion in foreign aid.

participating countries rose 162.6 percent, representing an average annual growth rate of 4.6 percent, compared with an average per capita growth rate in the United States of 1.6 percent during the same period. Europe's economic revival, of course, would not have been possible without the creativity, technical competence, and hard work of the European peoples involved. Nevertheless, by relieving shortages and boosting morale, the Marshall Plan was an important contribution.

For his enlightened statesmanship, George C. Marshall was awarded the Nobel Peace Prize in 1953. For the United States, too, the Marshall Plan brought enormous political as well as economic benefits. By creating jobs and raising individual incomes it checked the unease that menaced European political life. It thus stymied Soviet expansionism. Above all, the Marshall Plan created a sense of indebtedness and a reservoir of good feelings among Europeans toward the United States that later reinforced the Western military alliance system and U.S. leadership of the non-Communist nations. By stimulating European productivity and accepting a greater volume of imports, the United States saw its own exports increase markedly in the decades that followed.

The military dimension of the policy of containment was supplied by a resolution sponsored by Senator Vandenberg in June 1948. The Senate resolution called for "progressive development of regional and other collective arrangements for individual and collective self-defense in accordance with the purposes, principles, and provisions of the [United Nations] Charter." As early as September 1947, President Truman had signed such an agreement for Latin America. Signed by the United States and 18 other nations in the Western Hemisphere, the Inter-American Treaty of Reciprocal Assistance, or Rio Pact, declared that "an armed attack by any state shall be considered as an attack against all the American States and, consequently, each one of the said Contracting Parties undertakes to assist in meeting the attack." Signed in Washington in April 1949, the North Atlantic Treaty created the North Atlantic Treaty Organization (NATO) in order to safeguard the Atlantic community against the Soviet bloc (communist nations closely allied with the USSR). The Rio and NATO pacts ended the U.S. policy of avoiding entangling alliances. Economic aid and collective defense were the main instruments for containing the Soviet bloc.

With Dean Acheson presiding, European leaders gather in Washington, D.C., in April 1949, to announce the formation of the North Atlantic Treaty Organization (NATO). Acheson, secretary of state from 1947 to 1949, played a major part in forging the 10-nation alliance.

During the administration of Dwight D. Eisenhower (1953–61), the United States maintained the policy of containment, forming several regional alliances against the Soviet Union, including the Central Treaty Organization (CENTO), which involved Great Britain, Iran, Iraq, Pakistan, and Turkey; and the Southeast Asia Treaty (SEATO), which involved Australia, France, Great Britain, New Zealand, Pakistan, the Philippines, and Thailand. The country also entered bilateral treaties with Japan, South Korea, and the Republic of China on Taiwan. From time to time the United States fended off Communist thrusts. For example, when North Korea invaded South Korea in 1950, the United States sponsored a "police action" under the flag of the United Nations. The temporary Russian boycott of the United Nations Security Council enabled the United States to intervene through the organization (any one nation represented in the Security Council can veto military action). After a 3-year struggle the United Nations command, with the moral and some material support of 52 member nations, preserved the independence of South Korea in an unprecedented display of collective security.

Aware of the somewhat unwieldy structure of postwar foreign affairs agencies, Congress passed the National Security Act of 1947, which created the National Security Council (NSC) "to form and correlate national policy." The principal participants in the NSC, acting under the direction of the president, are the vice-president, the Joint Chiefs of Staff, and representatives of the Department of State, the Department of Defense, the Central Intelligence Agency, and, on occasion, interdepartmental groups. The creation of the NSC reflected the fact that few national security issues could be managed by a single agency. It did not displace the secretary of state as the president's senior adviser on foreign affairs. However, partly because international affairs represented a field in which the president could generally act more freely than in domestic affairs, the NSC gradually grew beyond the original concept of a deliberative, advisory body, and the head of the NSC, the national security adviser, a position not even mentioned in the 1947 act, sometimes competed with the secretary of state for influence on certain issues during the terms of Richard Nixon (1969–74), Jimmy Carter (1977–81), and Ronald Reagan (1981–88).

During the terms of Harry Truman (1945–53) and Dwight D. Eisenhower (1953–61), however, Secretaries of State George Marshall, Dean Acheson, John Foster Dulles, and Christian Herter enjoyed the full confidence and affirmative support of their chief executives. The sharp rise in the Department of State's responsibilities made it necessary that secretaries possess broad experience and technical skills. International lawyers were especially favored:

President Dwight D. Eisenhower (right) and his secretary of state John Foster Dulles (left foreground) attend a session of the UN General Assembly. Dulles expanded the free world alliance system through military and economic aid programs.

Acheson (1949–53), Dulles (1953–59), and Cyrus Vance (1977–80) exemplified this trend.

To accommodate the department's new activities its budget rose spectacularly: In 1940 the total expenditure was $24 million, but by 1950 it reached $350.9 million. After a decline in 1960, expenditures rose to $2.3 billion in 1980.

The McCarthy Era

In the first half of the 1950s the phenomenon of McCarthyism severely weakened the department. In February 1950, shortly after the Soviet Union acquired nuclear weapons and Mao Zedong seized power in China, Senator Joseph McCarthy of Wisconsin made a speech in Wheeling, West Virginia, in which he pictured the international status of the United States in calamitous terms. He concluded, "This must be the product of great conspiracy on a scale so immense as to dwarf any previous venture in the history of man." He claimed to have a list of 205 subversives—"a list of names that were made known to the Secretary of State as being members of the Communist Party and

Testifying before a congressional hearing, Senator Joseph McCarthy displays a map showing alleged centers of left-wing, or radical, activity. In February 1950, McCarthy began his reckless 4-year campaign against communism by charging that more than 200 State Department employees belonged to the Communist party.

who nevertheless are still working and shaping policy in the State Department." Although McCarthy never made public such a list nor proved any of his charges, numerous highly experienced Foreign Service officers—especially Far Eastern experts—were forced out of the department. The episode undoubtedly discouraged honest reporting and the airing of unpopular opinions even in the aftermath of McCarthy's decline, following a formal vote of censure by his Senate colleagues in 1954.

Détente

Trends in the 1950s and 1960s made diplomacy more complex than in the immediate postwar period. The achievement of freedom by many former colonies, the cooling of tensions between the Communist and non-Communist worlds, and the inconclusive introduction of 500,000 U.S. troops in Vietnam 10 years after the departure of the French in 1954 foreshadowed new directions in American foreign policy.

In February 1970, in collaboration with his assistant for national security affairs, Henry Kissinger, President Richard Nixon presented a document to Congress entitled *U.S. Foreign Policy for the 1970s*. He pointed to changes in the world scene since 1945: economic recovery; the birth of many new nations in Asia and Africa; the split in the unity of international communism in China and Eastern Europe; and the American loss of a monopoly on nuclear weapons. Nixon urged "heavy reliance on partnership with other nations; more emphasis on arms control and disarmament; and correction of the tendency to discount in advance the possibility of fruitful negotiations with Communist nations." In February 1972, Nixon visited Beijing, triggering a series of steps that ultimately led to normalization of relations with the People's Republic of China. In May 1972, he signed agreements in Moscow that contained the results of the first Strategic Arms Limitation Talks (SALT I). These events reflected a shift in American foreign policy from confrontation with the Communist powers to détente (a French term for reduced tension).

In spite of improved relations with the Soviet Union and Communist China, the international climate remained disturbed, especially in the economic

In Mai Linh, South Vietnam, a U.S. Army adviser (right) and a South Vietnamese soldier (left) plan a North Vietnam airstrike in 1972. North Vietnam and South Vietnam signed a peace pact in Paris in 1973, ending 12 years of American combat activity in Southeast Asia.

President Richard M. Nixon walks through China's Forbidden City (the palaces of former imperial rulers) in February 1972. Nixon's historic trip to the People's Republic of China was part of his administration's attempt to improve relations with the communist powers.

sphere. Since World War II other nations had calculated the value of their currencies relative to the U.S. dollar. In 1971, the dollar was devalued, leading to a period of unstable currency exchange rates. After the fourth Arab-Israeli War (October 1973), a group of Arab oil-producing nations (OPEC) boycotted oil shipments to important consumers in Europe and Asia. Henry Kissinger, appointed secretary of state in September 1973, spent much time trying to settle the long-running conflict between Israel and the Arab nations.

Under President Jimmy Carter (1977–81) the search went on for a formula to restore political stability in the Middle East. With the tireless brokering of President Carter and his State Department, in Maryland in September 1978 Prime Minister Menachem Begin of Israel and President Anwar Sadat of Egypt signed the so-called Camp David Accords, whereby the two governments agreed to return the Sinai Peninsula to Egypt and to negotiate Palestinian autonomy in the occupied West Bank and Gaza Strip. The Israelis had occupied this triangular peninsula near the Suez Canal since 1967. President Carter's most far-reaching imprint on foreign policy was his promotion of international human rights. Earlier in the 1970s, Congress had placed legal restrictions on economic and military assistance to governments that violated internationally accepted human rights.

Recent Years

The most recent product of the almost incessant call for a change in the professional attitude and practices of the Foreign Service is the Foreign Service Act of 1980. The act was the first comprehensive reorganization of the Foreign Service since 1946. The law established a new Senior Foreign Service (SFS) with appointments made strictly on the basis of merit; reaffirmed the "up or out" principle, whereby officers not promoted within a specified period must resign; established a Foreign Service Labor Relations Board to hear grievances; and applied personnel provisions of the law to the State Department, the International Development Cooperation Agency, the U.S. Information Agency, and those employees of the Departments of Commerce and Agriculture assigned to the separate field services of those agencies.

The American civil rights movement might be viewed as a domestic manifestation of the international human rights movement. Although women and members of minority groups had long been employed by the Department of State, they have been conspicuously underrepresented, especially in the higher ranks. As late as 1905 Assistant Secretary Frederick Van Dyne remarked: "The greatest obstacle to the employment of women as diplomatic agents is their well-known inability to keep a secret." The first woman Foreign Service officer was not appointed until 1922. Career women did not attain ambassadorial rank until after World War II. The first woman Foreign Service officer to be appointed a U.S. ambassador (Switzerland, 1953–57) was Frances E. Willis, who remains the only woman to have been named career ambassador, the highest rank in the Foreign Service.

Because of prevailing discriminatory attitudes, blacks have been similarly underrepresented in the department. A few political appointees of the 19th century were black: For example, the abolitionist Frederick Douglass became minister to Haiti in 1889. In 1925, Clifford R. Wharton became the first black to enter the Foreign Service, and he later served as minister to Romania and ambassador to Norway. Dr. Ralph Bunche became the first black division chief in the Department of State in 1945 and went on to win the Nobel Peace Prize in 1950 for his work in Palestine on behalf of the United Nations. Like women and blacks, Hispanics have also been inadequately represented through the present. The first Hispanic chief of mission was Romualdo Pacheco of California, who became minister to a group of Central American states in 1890.

Since the late 1960s, no issue has demanded more top-level attention than the increase in terrorism against official American representatives abroad. In

Frances Willis was named head of the American embassy in Switzerland in 1953, becoming the first woman member of the Foreign Service to be appointed as an ambassador.

After taking over the U.S. embassy in Iran on November 4, 1979, Islamic militants display blindfolded American hostages. The Iranians held the embassy employees for more than 14 months, agreeing to release them only after lengthy negotiations with Under Secretary of State Warren Christopher.

August 1968, Ambassador John Gordon Mein was assassinated in Guatemala, the first chief of mission to be murdered in the line of duty. Since then more U.S. ambassadors have been slain than U.S. generals lost since World War II.

On November 4, 1979, in the most dramatic act of terrorism against American diplomats, militant Islamic students seized the U.S. embassy in Iran and took its employees as hostages. The Iranian government refused to negotiate for the hostages' release, insisting that they were being held as punishment for the United States's support of the deposed ruler of Iran, the Shah. At the same time, American leaders refused to give in to the students' demands to return the Shah—who had fled the revolution and temporarily resided in the United States. A long stalemate ensued, during which the captured embassy employees were treated miserably. Isolated from each other in small rooms, often beaten, and given few sources of stimulation, many developed psychological disorders. On April 25, 1980, President Jimmy Carter sent a commando team into Iran to try to free the Americans. The mission ended in failure, however, after three American helicopters crashed in a sandstorm on the Iranian border. Angry with Carter's decision to use military force, Secretary of State Cyrus Vance resigned and was replaced by Edmund Muskie. As the hostage crisis dragged on, the American press gave it more and more attention and the American people became increasingly frustrated. In November 1981, Ronald Reagan defeated Carter in the race for the presidency, in large part because of Carter's failure to secure the release of the hostages. Finally, on January 20, 1981, the 52 hostages were let go after American negotiators, headed by Deputy Secretay of State Warren Christopher, agreed to release Iranian assets frozen in American banks and to give Iran a nonintervention pledge.

January 20, 1981, coincided with the presidential inauguration of Ronald Reagan, who quickly acted on his campaign pledge of a massive defense buildup. In dealing with the Soviet Union, Reagan was far more aggressive than

A battery of photographers descends on Lieutenant Colonel Oliver North, a National Security Council official, as he prepares to testify in July 1987 before a congressional committee investigating the Reagan administration's sale of arms to Iran and diversion of profits to Nicaraguan rebels.

his predecessors had been. Seeing the Soviet Union as an "evil empire," Reagan tried to check the rival superpower's influence in many regions, particularly Latin America. One example of Reagan's provocative approach was the 1983 U.S. invasion of the Caribbean Republic of Grenada. Claiming to be acting in defense of American medical students in Grenada, U.S. troops easily took the island and deposed its socialist regime.

Under Reagan, the United States also assumed a confrontational stance toward Libya. In April 1986, after a terrorist attack on a West Berlin disco frequented by American soldiers, the president ordered a bombing raid on the accused perpetrator, Libya, striking, among other spots, the headquarters of Libyan leader Muammar Qaddafi. This strike was the peak of the Reagan antiterrorist campaign. Less popular with the American people was the administration's effort to check possible Communist expansion in Nicaragua. Congress, responding to indications of deep division in American public opinion, refrained from giving substantial military aid to the U.S.-supported guerrillas fighting the Sandinista regime in Nicaragua. The revelation by a Lebanese magazine in November 1986 that the United States had been selling arms to Iran contrary to administration public pledges left a large question mark over foreign policy cooperation between Congress and the executive branch in the remaining months of the Reagan administration, especially regarding Latin America and Nicaragua, where the profits of Iranian arms sales were directed.

Secretary of State George Shultz chats with President Ronald Reagan in the Oval Office. The secretary of state—the senior cabinet officer—advises the president on foreign affairs, negotiates treaties, supervises American diplomats, and manages the State Department.

CHAPTER FIVE

In Washington: What the State Department Does

The structure of the State Department is perhaps more complicated than that of any other federal agency. This is not surprising considering that the department maintains missions in almost every country on earth and communicates and interacts daily with hundreds of other agencies, foreign governments, and international organizations.

Authority in the State Department radiates from its headquarters building in the Foggy Bottom area of Washington, D.C. Located on the seventh floor of this building are the offices of the department's top officials, who are sometimes referred to as the seventh-floor principals. This upper echelon consists of, in decreasing order of authority, the secretary of state, the deputy secretary of state, and five aides of under secretary rank—the counselor, the under secretary for security assistance, science and technology, the under secretary for political affairs, the under secretary for economic affairs, and the under secretary for management. The counselor assists the secretary of state on special projects—such as the negotiation of treaties and the preparation of crucial policy alliances.

Subordinate to the seventh-floor principals in the Washington office are an array of offices, bureaus, divisions, and special aides to the secretary. These can be broken down into the following categories:

—Independent officers with their own staffs: legal adviser and chief of protocol.

—In-house think tank: the Policy Planning Council

—Four independent agencies supervised by the secretary of state: the U.S. Information Agency, the Arms Control and Disarmament Agency, the Agency for International Development, and the International Development Cooperation Agency.

—Six regional bureaus: European and Canadian Affairs, East Asian and Pacific Affairs, African Affairs, Inter-American Affairs, Near Eastern and South Asian Affairs, and International Organization Affairs.

—Twelve functional bureaus: the Bureau of Intelligence and Research, Bureau of Consular Affairs, Bureau of Legislative and Intergovernmental Affairs, Political-Military Bureau, Bureau of Economic and Business Affairs, Bureau of Oceans and International Environmental and Scientific Affairs, Bureau of Human Rights and Humanitarian Affairs, Bureau of Refugee Programs, Bureau of International Narcotics Matters, Bureau of International Communication and Information Policy, Bureau of Diplomatic Security, and Bureau of Public Affairs.

—Administrative branch: Bureau of Administration, Personnel, Office for the Foreign Service, the Foreign Service Institute, the comptroller, the Office of Equal Opportunity and Civil Rights, and the inspector-general.

The structure of the department's overseas operations is less complex. There are two basic types of foreign posts—embassies and consulates. Embassies are run by ambassadors and consulates by consuls. These missions are staffed by members of the Foreign Service, officials from federal agencies other than the State Department, and citizens of the host countries.

Interactions between the Washington office and foreign posts occur through many different channels. Regional bureaus are the primary link between the headquarters and representatives abroad. But functional bureaus also frequently do business with foreign missions. For instance, if an ambassador or some other official at a foreign mission needs advice on a foreign policy dispute involving an environmental problem—for instance, acid rain—he will probably deal with the staff of the Bureau of Oceans and International Environmental and Scientific Affairs. Or if an ambassador is stationed in a nation that exports a large amount of illegal drugs to the United States, he or she will probably have occasion to work with the Bureau of International Narcotics Matters. Moreover, large embassies often have officials from several or all of the functional bureaus stationed on the premises.

Independent Officers

The legal adviser supplies expertise on domestic and international law to the secretary of state and other members of the State Department who solicit his aid. Among other duties, he interprets the legal language in treaties and agreements that the nation signs, attends international conferences on legal issues, provides American contributions in the codification of international law, represents the United States in international litigation, and works with the Justice Department on domestic cases involving the State Department. In recent years, the legal adviser and his staff have been in the national spotlight with increasing frequency. In 1987, Abraham Sofaer, the legal adviser under Secretary of State George Shultz, provided key testimony to congressional committees investigating the Reagan administration's sale of arms to Iran and

Abraham Sofaer (right), State Department legal adviser under Reagan, meets with the Egyptian foreign minister. The legal adviser carries out special diplomatic missions, interprets treaties, attends conferences on international law, and represents the United States in the World Court.

its illegal diversion of profits from those sales to Nicaraguan rebels known as Contras. Sofaer also put forth a controversial interpretation of the 1972 nuclear arms treaty with the Soviet Union, holding that the pact's restrictions on defensive weapons did not apply to the testing and development of the Reagan administration's proposed space-based defense system, known as the Strategic Defense Initiative (SDI), or Star Wars. And, in 1986, soon after Ferdinand Marcos was overthrown as leader of the Philippines, a member of Sofaer's staff spent a month with the former president, helping him determine the legal status of his massive investments around the world.

Another independent officer is the chief of protocol, who assists the president, vice-president, and secretary of state in matters pertaining to the internationally accepted rules of etiquette for official meetings and ceremonies with foreign leaders. He or she plans the ceremonial aspects of state visits by foreign leaders to this country, trips to other countries by the president and vice-president, and the presentation of credentials by foreign envoys to the president. (At the beginning of their tours of duty in the United States, all foreign diplomats formally present documentation from their governments demonstrating their right to serve as emissary.) In planning state functions, the chief of protocol must be aware of other nations' traditions regarding such matters as dietary restrictions and religious practices.

Policy Planning Council

The top leaders of the State Department are usually so busy with important meetings and various crises that they have no time to devote to foreign policy analysis. For this reason, in 1947 the department set up an in-house "think tank" called the Policy Planning Council. Composed of scholars, Foreign Service officers, and presidential appointees, the council analyzes current events in detail and develops long-range strategies for foreign policy. During the 1980s, the council prepared in-depth reports on such important international problems as growing unrest among Palestinians in Israel's occupied territories, the accumulation of massive foreign debts by Latin American countries, and the threat posed to the world oil supply by the war between Iran and Iraq. The council also assists American leaders in making decisions by outlining alternative courses of action for various foreign policy situations. Often the staff serves as the "devil's advocate" of the department, advancing arguments against certain policies and programs in order to examine their weaknesses and shortcomings. Finally, the council is charged with evaluating

Officials of the Agency for International Development (AID) distribute sacks of flour to needy Peruvians. The AID is one of four independent federal agencies affiliated with the State Department.

criticisms of American foreign policy that are made by members of the department through an unusual mechanism called the "dissent channel." Established in 1971 in response to widespread dissatisfaction in the department with America's involvement in Vietnam, the channel allows any officer to formally express opposition to American foreign policy by forwarding a memo to the Washington office.

Affiliated Agencies

Under the general guidance and direction of the secretary of state are four independent federal agencies: the U.S. Information Agency (USIA), which oversees the government's press, educational, and broadcasting operations abroad (including the Voice of America radio network); the Arms Control and Disarmament Agency, which does research and offers expert advice on limiting the world arms race; the Agency for International Development (AID), which administers nonmilitary foreign assistance programs; the International Development Cooperation Agency (IDCA), the umbrella agency for AID and the Overseas Private Investment Corporation, which offers risk insurance and other help to U.S. businesses abroad. The IDCA also supervises U.S. economic relations with developing countries.

Although these agencies function most of the time as independent bodies, on matters of great importance their directors are obligated to consult the Department of State. And the secretary of state can mobilize their resources for his own purposes whenever he wishes. For instance, in 1983, after the Soviet Union shot down a Korean Air Lines jet that strayed over Soviet territory, State Department officials ordered the USIA to utilize its information network to rouse international indignation over the incident. Similarly, the secretary has on several occasions ordered AID to cancel economic assistance to nations whose political systems are considered threatening to the United States.

The Regional Bureaus

The six bureaus in this category are the most direct links between the State Department and American embassies. As such, they are often referred to as the heart of the department. There are bureaus for the following areas: African Affairs, Inter-American Affairs, East Asian and Pacific Affairs, European and Canadian Affairs, Near Eastern and South Asian Affairs, and International Organization Affairs. Each is headed by an assistant secretary, who has primary responsibility for working out policies toward and conducting routine relations with foreign countries in his or her area.

For each country with which the United States maintains relations, there is a country officer, who is usually the first person to see a communication coming in from an American embassy. He has the option of dealing with the matter independently or referring it to his superior, the assistant secretary. Officially accountable for all embassy activities in his region, the assistant secretary also acts as a conduit for messages going to embassies from the secretary of state.

The above description applies only to the five regional bureaus that supervise American embassies. The sixth, the Bureau of International Organization Affairs, oversees the American mission to the United Nations (UN) in New York City, manages American delegations to specialized UN agencies located abroad, and organizes American participation in about 800 international conferences every year. Unlike the other five regional bureaus, which concentrate on bilateral relations (relations between the United States and one other country), the Bureau of International Organization Affairs primarily handles multilateral activities (those involving more than two nations). The bureau also supervises American delegations at the UN's specialized agencies for agriculture, atomic energy, labor, and other fields.

The United States plays an important role in the United Nations. In addition to participating in the General Assembly, the United States belongs—along with France, Great Britain, the People's Republic of China, and the Soviet Union—to the permanent body of the UN Security Council. It also pays about a quarter of the international body's annual expenses. (Federal funds for the UN are channeled through the State Department and constitute about half of State's budget.) The head of the U.S. mission to the UN is called the ambassador to the United Nations. In recent years, this position has been filled by such luminaries as Andrew Young, who helped the Carter administration win greater support among Third World nations, and Jeane Kirkpatrick, who had a strong influence on the Reagan administration's hard-line stance toward socialist nations in Latin America.

Andrew Young, U.S. ambassador to the UN under President Carter, addresses fellow UN delegates. The American mission to the UN is overseen by the State Department's Bureau of International Organization Affairs.

Harold Brown, left, President Carter's secretary of defense, whispers to Secretary of State Cyrus Vance during testimony before the Senate Foreign Relations Committee. The Bureau of Legislative and Intergovernmental Affairs arranges congressional appearances by State Department officials.

Functional Bureaus

Bureau of Legislative and Intergovernmental Affairs. No part of the federal government is more vital to the department's success than Congress. The legislative body makes important decisions regarding the department's administration—approving its budget, reviewing high-level appointments, and, on occasion, making changes in its organizational structure. Congress also serves as a partner—and sometimes an adversary—to the State Department and the president in establishing the nation's foreign policy. To manage the department's relations with Congress, the Bureau of Legislative and Intergovernmental Affairs was established after World War II. The bureau's most important function is to present the department's legislative agenda to the Senate and the House of Representatives. Other tasks include arranging for senior department officials to appear before congressional committees and subcommittees, organizing regular briefings on department activities for lawmakers, and advising other branches of the department on congressional matters. In addition, the bureau's staff responds to the thousands of letters the department receives every year from senators and representatives.

Bureau of Intelligence and Research. The Department of State is a member of the American intelligence community, a group of federal agencies that, as at least part of their function, collect and analyze intelligence (information on military, economic, and political conditions in foreign countries). Within the department, responsibility for gathering intelligence lies primarily with the Bureau of Intelligence and Research. Unfettered by current departmental or national foreign policy, bureau analysts file frequent appraisals of developments overseas. Each day, a summary of their findings—called the Secretary's Daily Intelligence Summary—is distributed among top State Department officers. The bureau also serves as the department's liaison to the American intelligence community—which includes the Central Intelligence Agency, the Department of Defense, the National Security Council, Army Intelligence, Navy Intelligence, Air Force Intelligence, the National Reconnaissance Office, the Federal Bureau of Investigation, the Drug Enforcement Administration, the Department of Energy, and the Department of the Treasury.

Bureau of Consular Affairs. The Bureau of Consular Affairs is the State Department's oldest bureau. It was established as one of the seven original bureaus during Secretary Louis McLane's reorganization of the department in 1833. Today it performs the same functions it always has—overseeing American consulates and consular officers at embassies and providing consular service for Americans in the United States.

The bureau's Citizens Emergency Center helps people in the United States who have a relative missing abroad or a family emergency that requires that a relative abroad be notified. People who need such services can telephone the office in Washington at 202-647-5225 to request a "welfare-and-whereabouts" search. The emergency center also assists in the transfer of private funds—when there is no commercial channel available—and issues travel advisories warning of conditions abroad that are likely to adversely affect traveling Americans.

The Bureau of Consular Affairs's second major service for people in the United States is providing passports for foreign travel. One out of every 10 Americans holds a U.S. passport issued by the bureau. A passport is an

The Bureau of Consular Affairs provides two major public services for Americans at home: Its Citizens Emergency Center helps U.S. residents locate relatives or friends who are missing overseas and its 13 regional offices issue passports such as the one pictured here.

internationally recognized travel document attesting to the identity and nationality of the bearer. It indicates that its bearer is entitled to receive the protection and assistance of the diplomatic and consular officers of his or her country while abroad. It is also a request by the issuing government that officials of foreign governments permit the bearer to travel in their territories and afford him or her all lawful aid and protection. In 1987, the Consular Bureau's 13 regional passport offices in the United States issued nearly 5 million passports.

Bureau of Public Affairs. The main responsibility of this bureau is handling relations with the press in the United States. (Officials of the United States Information Agency deal with reporters at American posts abroad.) At least once a day—and sometimes more frequently—the bureau holds briefings for the media at State Department headquarters. The head of the bureau, who has the titles of assistant secretary for public affairs and spokesperson for the department, delivers all major announcements and voices official reactions to overseas events. The department prides itself on being one of the most open foreign ministries in the world. More than 800 television, radio, and newspaper reporters, American and foreign, hold press passes for the State Department building. Much of the significant material generated in daily press conferences is reprinted by the bureau in the monthly magazine *Department of State* and the yearbook *American Foreign Policy: Current Documents*. Other important foreign affairs publications distributed by the bureau include the *Background Notes* series, concise summaries of political and economic conditions in more than 150 countries, and *Foreign Relations of the United States*, an ongoing documentary history of American diplomacy.

Political-Military Bureau (PM). This bureau handles State Department relations with the Department of Defense—the executive department with which State most often interacts. The director of the bureau, who has the rank of assistant secretary, keeps State Department officials apprised of Defense Department positions on foreign policy. He is also the secretary of state's chief adviser on all matters where defense and foreign policy overlap. At the same time, bureau staff members analyze the political consequences of military

State Department spokesman Charles Redman makes an announcement to the press. The Bureau of Public Affairs conducts such briefings and also distributes hundreds of pamphlets and books on foreign policy.

actions proposed by the Department of Defense. For instance, the bureau often comments to the Department of Defense on the timing of proposed visits by U.S. naval vessels to foreign ports. Docking armed ships in a foreign nation's port at the wrong time can sometimes create ill-will.

The Political-Military Bureau also works with the Department of Defense to coordinate the federal government's sale and provision of military equipment to foreign nations. Although the Defense Department's Defense Security Agency actually administers the military assistance program, the PM performs the complex task of preparing the program's budget for presentation to Congress. Much of the cooperation between the PM and the Defense Department takes place in the National Security Council (NSC), especially in the NSC Political-Military Interdepartmental Group (a committee that is chaired by the PM's director). Through the NSC, PM officials are given an opportunity to review the Defense Department's budget and to comment on basic military policy papers, such as the secretary of defense's annual report to Congress.

In cooperation with the Department of Commerce, the PM's Office of Munitions Control regulates the sale of arms by private manufacturers and dealers to foreign clients.

Bureau of Economic and Business Affairs. When it was created after World War II, this bureau's primary function was to promote trade between American firms and foreign companies. In recent years, however, it has lost much of its responsibility in this realm to other federal agencies. In 1963 the position of the U.S. Trade Representative was created in the executive office of the president and given final authority over American foreign trade. And in 1979, primary responsibility for promoting business at overseas posts was transferred from the economic bureau to the Department of Commerce. Nevertheless, the bureau continues to play an important role in trade promotion. It works with managers of American companies to increase their exports. It tries to resolve disputes between American and foreign companies over patents, trademarks, copyrights, and restrictive business practices. And, in conjunction with the Commerce and Treasury departments, it is negotiating revisions of the 1947 General Agreement on Trade and Tariffs (GATT)—the only major international agreement establishing rules for trade.

In addition to trade promotion, the bureau assists American firms in establishing branches overseas, and it helps the State Department exert influence in the formulation of American foreign economic policy. It helps ensure that American multinational corporations (businesses with headquarters in one country and affiliates in others) follow accepted codes of conduct and, when applicable, American law.

Bureau of Oceans and International Environmental and Scientific Affairs (OES). The bureau was created in 1973 as a combination of the former Bureau of International Scientific and Technological Affairs and the offices of the coordinator of ocean affairs, the special assistant for wildlife and fisheries, and the special assistant for environmental affairs. Its primary duty is to develop America's foreign policy regarding oceanic, scientific, and environmental issues. Under a 1978 law, the bureau—as the surrogate of the secretary of state—is charged with coordinating all scientific and technological cooperation between the United States and other countries. Bureau officials represent the United States at dozens of annual international scientific conferences, committees, and negotiations. As of 1987, the bureau maintained 42 full-time and 100 part-time attachés at American missions overseas.

The 1978 act also charged the bureau with monitoring the nation's compliance with the more than 100 international and environmental pacts it has entered. For instance, the bureau enforces the Antarctic Treaty, a 1959 agreement by which 35 countries, including the United States, pledged to preserve the icy continent as a zone of peace. In recent years, as the world's nations have become increasingly aware of the damage man has wrought to the environment, OES has represented the United States in international efforts to reduce pollution and protect global natural resources.

The bureau is currently engaged in a joint project with the Canadian government to reduce acid rain in common border areas. The bureau is also participating in an international campaign to preserve the ozonosphere, a gaseous layer of the atmosphere that helps shield the earth from dangerous solar radiation. In the last several decades, the ozone layer has been severely depleted by the proliferation of chlorofluorocarbons, which are released from aerosol sprays and other man-made substances. In accordance with an international agreement concluded at the 1985 Vienna Convention for the Protection of the Ozone Layer, OES cooperates with other nations in researching, monitoring, and exchanging data on the problem. Since entering the agreement, the bureau has had considerable success in convincing American companies to curtail production of chlorofluorocarbons and in arousing public awareness about the dangers of ozone depletion.

Bureau of Human Rights and Humanitarian Affairs (HA). This bureau was established by President Jimmy Carter in 1977 as part of his campaign to reduce political repression abroad. Its main function is to prepare annual reports on human rights conditions in all countries that receive aid from the United States and all countries that belong to the United Nations. These reports are used by federal officials in deciding each year whether or not to continue foreign aid programs. A law passed by Congress in early 1972 forbids American aid to countries that engage "in a consistent pattern of gross violations of internationally recognized human rights." As defined by Congress, human rights include freedom from torture; freedom from cruel, inhuman, or degrading treatment or punishment; freedom from prolonged detention without charges; and the right to life, liberty, and security.

The bureau also cooperates with the Justice Department in the processing of requests for political asylum (permission granted to foreign citizens to live in the United States to escape political repression in their home nations). Although the Justice Department's Immigration and Naturalization Service makes the final decision on all requests, HA submits advisory reports on the applications of many refugees.

A demonstration in Buenos Aires in support of two citizens who were declared "disappeared" by Argentina's right-wing rulers, but who were most likely murdered. Annual reports on such abuses prepared by the Bureau of Human Rights and Humanitarian Affairs are used by American leaders in determining whether to continue aid programs.

Bureau of Refugee Programs. Like HA, the Bureau of Refugee Programs was established by the Carter administration to address a pressing international problem—in this case, the recent growth of the world's refugee population. As defined by the 1951 Geneva Convention (one of a series of international treaties establishing rules for the humane treatment of combatants and civilians in wartime), refugees are people who live outside their country of "habitual residence who cannot or will not return . . . because of a well-founded fear of persecution on account of race, religion or nationality or membership in a particular social group." The Bureau of Refugee Programs works with other nations to help repatriate (return to their native land) refugees or assist them in settling in new countries. For the million refugees who the United States has admitted since 1975, the bureau arranges resettlement programs, provides job training and placement, and administers income subsidies and medical assistance. Often it contracts with private church and welfare organizations to provide these services.

The bureau also prepares an annual report on the refugee problem—*World Refugee Report*—which the House and Senate judiciary committees use in considering the president's proposals for admitting refugees. Nine percent of the State Department's budget goes to refugee programs—part of it to the Bureau of Refugee Programs and part to UN refugee programs, such as the UN Relief and Works Agency.

Bureau of International Narcotics Matters. Over the past 20 years, the flow of illegal drugs into the United States has risen substantially, leading to increases in violent crime and drug abuse. In an attempt to reduce the drug trade, federal officials have stepped up pressure on foreign governments to combat drug production and export. The Bureau of International Narcotics Matters was created to help wage this campaign, in close cooperation with the Drug Enforcement Administration, AID, and other federal agencies. With funds appropriated by Congress in the Foreign Assistance Act, the bureau assists foreign governments in curtailing narcotics production. As of 1987, 14 countries received funding, equipment, and personnel from the bureau for use in the eradication of opium poppies and other crops from which drugs are manufactured.

Bureau of International Communications and Technology. In recent years, telecommunications systems—radio, television, satellite communications, long-distance telephone networks, international computer linkages—have taken on increasing importance for the United States. In part, this is because they have become the foundation of the American economy. As of 1987, 60 percent of American workers had information-related jobs. Information and

These Southeast Asian poppies will eventually be harvested, shipped to another part of the world, and then processed to produce heroin. The State Department's Bureau of International Narcotics Matters works with other nations to reduce international drug trafficking.

telecommunications equipment now makes up a significant portion of American exports. Communications systems have also become central to the United States's interactions with foreign governments. Remarkable advances in technology now enable American leaders to keep track of and react instantly to events taking place all over the globe.

Established in 1985, the Bureau of International Communications and Technology is grappling with the implications of these trends for American foreign policy. The bureau helps ensure that American communication networks interact smoothly with foreign networks. This task is made especially difficult because American communications networks are privately owned, whereas many foreign ones are operated by governments. The bureau represents American communications companies in the International Telecommunications Agency, an international organization that, among other responsibilities, registers satellites and assigns broadcast frequencies. Bureau officials also attend international conferences on communications. A particularly urgent concern of the bureau is to help establish rules and regulations to govern the movement of data across national boundaries via computer networks.

Bureau of Diplomatic Security. The department's youngest bureau was created in 1986 in response to a marked increase in terrorist attacks against American diplomats and diplomatic installations over the previous 10 years. (Between 1976 and 1986, 36 names were added to the memorial plaque in the lobby of the department dedicated to employees of State and other foreign affairs agencies who have been killed in the line of duty.) Part of a $4.4 billion program to improve diplomatic security, the bureau supplies security officers to American embassies and consulates. It also develops design standards for new embassies aimed at reducing the possiblity of terrorist attack and infiltration by spies. It is involved in attempts to improve security for diplomats

A military sentry stands guard while journalists tour the new American embassy in the USSR, which had to be torn down and rebuilt midway through its construction because of extensive bugging by the Soviets. The Bureau of Diplomatic Security helps protect embassies against acts of espionage.

in the United States—visiting foreign officials, employees of international organizations, and personnel at embassies. The bureau is also the home base for the department's team of diplomatic couriers—63 men and women who travel the globe hand-delivering packages and letters considered too urgent or sensitive to be sent by mail.

Administration

The department's administrative wing is headed by the under secretary for management and includes the Bureau of Administration, the comptroller, the Office of Equal Opportunity and Civil Rights, an inspector-general, and the administrative offices of the Foreign Service and the Foreign Service Institute. Headed by the assistant secretary for adminstration, the Bureau of Administration disburses funds appropriated by Congress to the various divisions of the department, supervises interdepartmental communications, and acquires and maintains foreign buildings used as embassies, consular offices, and residences for Foreign Service personnel. The bureau also handles requests for the release of documents under the Freedom of Information Act. The FOIA gives "any person," including foreign nationals, access to all records of all federal agencies, excepting data on visa cases, trade secrets, information provided by foreign governments, and national security documents.

The comptroller is the money manager for the State Department and the Foreign Service. Reporting directly to the under secretary for management, he organizes the preparation of the department's budget. He is also responsible for payroll, accounting, and the payment of vendors.

The Foreign Service Institute offers instruction in special skills needed in the service, including about 40 foreign languages, orientation to various geographical areas, and courses for spouses on adjusting to overseas living.

The Office of Equal Opportunity and Civil Rights (OEOCR) is responsible for increasing the number of women and minorities in the department. As of September 30, 1986, these groups made up a relatively low proportion of the Foreign Service: 21.7 percent of Foreign Service officers were women and 12.1 percent were members of minority groups. In an attempt to convince more members of minority groups to take the Foreign Service exam, the equal opportunity office places advertisements with newspapers and radio stations and holds conferences with leaders from minority and women's organizations. For members of minorities who are already in the Foreign Service, the office provides career counseling. An inspector-general and a staff of FSOs and civil servants investigate alleged wrongdoing, audit accounts, and evaluate administrative practices and political and economic reporting. In order to help ensure objectivity, the inspector-general is by law a senior officer recruited from outside the Foreign Service itself. This officer reports directly to the secretary of state but also submits formal reports to Congress twice a year, and can be dismissed only by the president.

The Foreign Service Personnel System

The principal officer in Washington for the Foreign Service is the director general of the Foreign Service. This officer also serves as the director of personnel, overseeing the recruitment, assignment, and promotion of the department's Foreign Service officers, Civil Service employees, and Foreign Service nationals. The Foreign Service is a pool of career diplomats from which the State Department fills the majority of skilled positions at American missions overseas. The service claims about 9,200 members—4,200 Foreign Service officers and 5,000 secretaries, communications technicians, and other specialists. About 40 percent of the service's officers work for the State Department in Washington, at all levels from assistant desk officer to under secretary. Overseas they serve at all levels from attaché to ambassador.

Entrance into the Foreign Service is competitive. More than 16,000 men and women take the Foreign Service examination every year. The screening process is extremely demanding and involves several steps. First applicants take a day-long written test, which includes an essay portion and a multiple-choice section that measure knowledge of geography, international relations, American cultural history, and basic scientific and management principles. Those who pass the written test are given an oral assessment—which includes a 45-minute oral examination to test knowledge of current political, economic, and cultural issues; a group exercise with other applicants; and two essays.

At the end of the evaluation process, about 200 to 225 of the original applicants finally enter the service. All new members of the service receive their first assignment overseas, most of them as consular officers issuing visas and helping American citizens abroad.

Subsequently, they are given assignments in one of four "cones," or specialties—administrative, economic, political, or public affairs. In 4 or 5 years, 85 percent of the original class of 200 to 250 become full-fledged Foreign Service officers. After meeting language requirements, these officers begin moving toward senior positions. Each stage of advancement is competitive. To

Foreign Service officers attend a Spanish class at the Foreign Service Institute. Established in 1946 and run by the administrative wing of the Foreign Service, the institute provides instruction in more than 40 languages.

be promoted to the upper ranks, officers must show the ability to run complex programs. It is also advantageous to demonstrate expert knowledge of one or two difficult languages (for example, Russian, Chinese, Japanese, or Arabic). Fifty percent of each entering "class" is eventually promoted to the 670-member Senior Foreign Service, from which the top positions in Washington and the embassies and consulates are filled. Three or four members of each class are eventually promoted to the rank of ambassador or assistant secretary of state.

Civil Service

Approximately 4,500 civil servants are permanently assigned to the Department of State's Washington headquarters, 13 passport offices, and other State facilities around the country. This group comprises 42 percent of the department's total work force. They are employed as attorneys, engineers, and linguists, and they fill the majority of administrative and secretarial positions. One hundred and twenty of them belong to the Senior Executive Service, the elite corps of United States-based government workers.

The U.S. embassies in Prague, Czechoslovakia (top), and Riyadh, Saudi Arabia (bottom). Headed by ambassadors appointed by the president, staffed by officials from several federal agencies, and overseen by the State Department, American embassies handle day-to-day political and economic relations with other nations.

SIX

Overseas: What American Embassies and Consulates Do

The basic unit for the conduct of American diplomacy abroad is the embassy. An embassy, strictly speaking, is the staff of an ambassador. Appointed by the president and confirmed by the Senate, an ambassador is the personal representative of the chief executive to another head of state. He or she also receives instructions from the secretary of state in the latter's role as principal foreign affairs adviser to the president. Nevertheless, for the government and people of the country where he or she serves, the ambassador is the embodiment of the United States of America. As of 1987, 60 percent of U.S. ambassadors were drawn from the Foreign Service. The rest were political appointees from other walks of life: business, education, electoral politics, labor organizations, and state governments.

The ambassador's closest associate is the deputy chief of mission, who is always an experienced member of the Foreign Service. Below that level, the embassy is organized into functional sections. Most embassies have four sections—political, economic, consular, and administrative. Sections are staffed by many types of officials: State Department officials who belong to the

Foreign Service, State Department officials who belong to the Civil Service (who are assigned overseas only on a temporary basis), political appointees of the State Department, officers from other federal agencies and departments, and foreign employees (Foreign Service nationals). Approximately 30 government agencies, from the Coast Guard to the Library of Congress, have employees in U.S. embassies.

In the spring of 1987 the United States had diplomatic relations with 155 countries. An American ambassador (or chief of mission of lesser rank) represented the United States in the majority of these nations. In a few small countries where the United States had no official presence, contacts were maintained through embassies in neighboring countries or through the United Nations. The United States had no diplomatic relations with Albania, Angola, Cambodia, Cuba, Iran, North Korea, and South Yemen (Aden).

Although there can be only one U.S. embassy per country, located in the capital, there may be numerous subordinate posts called consulates or consulates-general. (The latter are simply large consulates.) The principal officer at a consulate, called the consul, is the ranking representative of the Foreign Service in the consular district. Although he or she works for the ambassador, the consul has authority to report directly to the department whenever he or she considers it appropriate (for example, in regard to an unexpected election result, an assassination, or a difficult visa case.) Consulates have the same basic sections as embassies—political, economic, consular, and administrative—but the work load is usually weighted in favor of consular work. Like embassies, consulates are usually staffed by members of several government agencies in addition to the Department of State. At some large consulates-general, as many as 12 other agencies may be represented.

The Country Team

Activities at many embassies are coordinated by management panels called "country teams." Chaired by the ambassador, a country team usually consists of representatives from each federal agency represented at the mission. However, because country teams have no legislative basis, there are no formal rules for their composition or function. The frequency with which they meet and the relative authority they wield varies greatly from mission to mission. At country team meetings, members might discuss such topics as a coup d'état (overthrow of the government) in the host nation, the suitability of a proposed site for an American information library, or predictions for the outcome of an upcoming election.

Ambassador Helene von Damm presides over a country team meeting at the U.S. embassy in Geneva, Switzerland. Consisting of the top officers of each embassy section, country teams help ambassadors coordinate activities at foreign missions.

The Four Traditional Sections of an Embassy or Consulate

The Political Section. Political officers analyze and report on political matters in the host nation. They also convey U.S. government views on political issues to foreign officials, negotiate political agreements, and maintain close contact with local politicians, labor leaders, and third-country diplomats. In a typical week, an overseas political officer might report on a foreign election, draft remarks for a visiting congressman, and report to Washington on the visit of an American delegation. Most political section employees are members of the Foreign Service. As such, they usually remain in a position for only a few years, because of the service's system of rotating its personnel from post to post. Nevertheless, they usually manage to become specialists in a certain country or region.

The Economic Section. Economic officers analyze and report on economic

Giving her trademark two-finger salute, Filipino politician Corazon Aquino campaigns for the presidency prior to the 1986 ouster of the long-time leader of the Philippines, Ferdinand Marcos. Among other duties, political officers at U.S. embassies monitor foreign elections.

trends and events that affect U.S. interests. They gather and interpret data, present U.S. economic positions to foreign officials, and negotiate agreements, both bilaterally and multilaterally. They keep in close touch with foreign business representatives, bankers, and economists and cultivate close ties with American investors and exporters. They also monitor oil and gas production and prices and seek foreign support for American economic initiatives at the United Nations.

At larger embassies, the economic section also includes science attachés, who communicate with the local scientific community, present American views on international scientific and environmental issues, observe joint scientific programs, and monitor scientific discoveries. In about 40 countries, labor attachés are assigned to either the economic or political sections. Labor attachés observe labor standards abroad and study foreign labor unions. The International Bureau of the Department of Labor in Washington receives their reports and circulates many of their findings to interested groups in the United States—such as the American Federation of Labor and Congress of Industrial Organizations (AFL-CIO) and U.S. businesses with overseas operations.

The Administrative Section. Administrative officers arrange for housing, hire local national employees, and operate and maintain word processing and computer equipment and the sophisticated communication machinery connecting embassies and consulates with Washington and each other. The administrative section in a present-day post may vary in size from a single officer supervising a few nationals hired in the host country to 20–30 Americans and several hundred foreign citizens. The size of the section will normally be

Arms instructors teach secretaries at the U.S. embassy in Beirut, Lebanon, how to fire a pistol. State Department security officers provide such training to employees of embassies in politically turbulent regions.

determined by the total number of U.S. employees for whom the embassy provides services. The section supports all employees attached to the mission, even those who are not affiliated with the Department of State. (Every year the State Department is reimbursed for the portion of its administrative expenses that are spent on supporting representatives of other agencies.)

Also assigned to administrative sections are security officers from the Bureau of Diplomatic Security. In recent years, with the rise in terrorist acts against American diplomats, security efforts at American embassies and consulates have been increased considerably. Between 1985 and 1987, the number of security officers in the field doubled. In fact, at some embassies located in especially turbulent areas, separate sections have been set up for security personnel. For the most part, security officers act as security advisers and supervisors, determining ways to combat espionage and to secure

A member of the U.S. Marine Corps mans his station at the U.S. embassy in Amman, Jordan. About 1,300 Marines serve as security guards at American embassies around the world.

embassies against terrorist attacks. They also manage the State Department's fleet of armored vehicles and organize special training teams to provide self-defense instruction to diplomats stationed in high-risk areas. They do not, however, serve as embassy security guards. That task is left to detachments from the U.S. Marine Corps. In 1987, 1,300 Marine security guards were assigned to 140 posts around the world.

Finally, mention must be made of Narcotic Assistance Officers, Foreign Service officers operating under separate legal authority in Mexico, Columbia, Peru, Bolivia, Brazil, Ecuador, Turkey, Pakistan, Burma, Thailand, the Bahamas, and Jamaica. These officers work closely with representatives of the Drug Enforcement Administration and the host government to design and carry out programs aimed at improving local customs service, reducing drug production, and preventing drug abuse.

The Consular Section. Consular officers at consulates and embassies have been called the U.S. government's human face because they provide services to millions of people every year. These services can be broken down into two general categories: visas for foreign citizens and services for American citizens abroad.

Visas: U.S. law requires that both temporary visitors and people who intend to immigrate obtain visas (permits) before traveling to the United States. The processing and issuance of visas constitute the main work load of a consular section; roughly two-thirds of all consular officers deal with visa issues. In 1987, the Department of State issued nearly 7 million nonimmigrant (temporary visitor) visas and 390,000 immigrant visas. It is important to note that the visa allows a person only to apply to enter the United States. At the port of entry, the U.S. Immigration and Naturalization Service makes the final decision on whether or not a visa holder may enter the United States. U.S. immigration law spells out in detail who can qualify for an immigrant visa or for one of several types of nonimmigrant—for example, visitor, student, or temporary worker—visas. However, whether or not an applicant qualifies under law for a visa is a judgment that a consular officer must make.

Services to American citizens abroad: Today more American citizens are traveling, studying, and doing business in other countries than at any other time in U.S. history. In 1986, more than 14 million Americans traveled abroad and, with more than 6,000 American firms maintaining offices outside the United States, there is a tremendous need to assist U.S. citizens who get into trouble overseas. Americans abroad may turn to a U.S. embassy or consulate when they become ill, need money, need tax information, fail to receive Social

American children who live with their families in France attend class at a French school. Americans living or traveling abroad may receive help from U.S. consulates in a variety of situations—such as when they need tax information, run out of money, lose their passports, or become ill.

Security checks, are arrested, lose their passports, are robbed, or have a family member disappear.

In 1987, more than 3,000 Americans were arrested abroad; 41 percent of those were arrested on drug charges. A consular officer cannot get a U.S. citizen out of jail, but he or she will visit the U.S. citizen in jail, supply a list of local lawyers, make every effort to see that the prisoner is treated fairly and humanely under local law in accordance with international standards, and, if the arrested person wishes, will notify friends or relatives in the United States of the detainee's condition.

Programs of Affiliated Agencies

The staff of nearly every American embassy includes officers from the U.S. Information Service (USIS), the overseas arm of the U.S. Information Agency, one of the independent agencies affiliated with the State Department. The ranking USIS officer in each country, the public affairs officer, acts as the ambassador's principal adviser on press and public relations and is often the embassy spokesperson. Lower-level information officers handle relations with the media of the host country, provide assistance to American journalists stationed there, and arrange press conferences for visiting American officials. The information service also supplies many embassies and consulates with cultural affairs officers who administer educational and cultural exchange programs, organize exhibits by American artists, manage libraries, and help local publishers with translations of American books.

Representatives of a second agency affiliated with the State Department, the Agency for International Development (AID), are stationed at embassies in most of the 77 countries that receive American economic aid. These officers administer economic grants, loans, and technical assistance (for example, training in industrial techniques and the management of farm cooperatives).

Programs of Other Agencies

Many other federal departments and agencies also have personnel assigned to embassies. Since 1979, members of the Commerce Department's foreign arm, the Foreign Commercial Service (FCS), have had the primary responsibility at embassies for promoting international trade. Officers of the FCS conduct market research for American firms, resolve trade disputes, help link American manufacturers with foreign distributors, and operate export development offices. In the area of agricultural trade promotion, Commerce Department representatives are assisted by the Department of Agriculture's foreign arm, the Foreign Agricultural Service, which has officers in more than 60 countries. In addition to promoting trade, FAS attachés help foreign nations develop programs to control pests that might endanger American crops; they also chart the success of foreign farmers, and cooperate with AID officials to improve the productivity of foreign agriculture.

Next to the State Department, the Defense Department has the largest number of employees in embassies—more than 4,100. Many of these men and women serve as defense attachés who report to the Defense Intelligence Agency and do for military affairs what political and economic officers do in their spheres: report on and analyze developments affecting the military in their countries of assignment and advise the ambassador on issues in their fields of expertise. In about 50 countries, the Department of Defense has Military Assistance Advisory Groups (MAAGs), which administer American military assistance to foreign nations and provide combat training.

Special Missions

Although most Foreign Service officers work in embassies or at the Washington headquarters of the State Department, some are assigned to international organizations, commissions, or special peace-keeping missions. A few of the officers on these special assignments work for bilateral bodies such as the U.S.-Mexican International Boundary and Water Commission. The majority, however, are with American missions to the following multilateral international organizations: the United Nations, New York City; the Organization of American States, Washington, D.C.; the International Atomic Energy Agency, Vienna, Austria; the North Atlantic Treaty Organization, Brussels, Belgium; the Organization for Economic Cooperation and Development, Paris, France; the International Civil Aviation Organization, Montreal, Canada; the Mission to

A Peace Corps volunteer checks an expectant mother's blood pressure at a mother-child health care center in Niger. The Peace Corps is one of more than 45 federal agencies with personnel stationed abroad.

the European Communities (the Common Market), Brussels; the European Ofice of the United Nations and other International Organizations, Geneva, Switzerland; the Mission to United Nations Agencies for Food and Agriculture, Rome Italy; and an observer mission to the United Nations Educational, Scientific, and Cultural Organization, Paris.

In a few special cases, Foreign Service officers are stationed in countries where the United States does not have diplomatic relations. In such cases, another nation has taken charge of U.S. property in that country, and State Department personnel there are considered part of the embassy staff of the protecting power. For example, since 1977 the United States has had a Special Interest Section in the Swiss embassy in Havana, Cuba.

Diplomatic Privileges and Responsibilities

American diplomats enjoy the same legal privileges that all other nations' diplomats do. Under an agreement concluded at the 1961 Vienna Convention on Diplomatic Relations, which was ratified by more than 113 nations, diplomats are immune from arrest, subpoena (a writ requiring a person to appear in court), and, in many cases, taxation. The agreement also stipulates that embassies cannot be entered or searched without permission. These rules may at times seem absurd. For instance, foreign firemen trying to save a burning embassy must obtain official clearance before entering the premises. But such rules are necessary to protect the lives and property of diplomats—especially those assigned to hostile or war-torn nations.

Foreign Service Nationals

A little known fact about the Department of State is that almost 40 percent (about 10,000) of all its employees are not American citizens. (If part-time employees are counted, the percentage comes to nearly half the total workforce.) These foreign workers are called Foreign Service nationals. They are employed by embassies, consulates, and other State Department installations to fill such positions as cook, maid, gardener, chauffeur, computer technician, and political adviser. At times quesitons have been raised about the wisdom of relying so heavily upon people whose first allegiance probably belongs to other governments. But with few exceptions Foreign Service nationals have provided excellent service.

At the Camp David presidential retreat, Cyrus Vance (left) and Zbigniew Brzezinski (right), President Carter's national security adviser, work into the night on a pressing foreign policy problem. In the age of nuclear weapons and interconnected economies, the State Department's task of managing the nation's foreign policy is a challenging—and sometimes exhausting—one.

SEVEN

Practicing an Inexact Science in an Untidy World

Jules Jusserand, the French ambassador to the United States from 1902 to 1925, once defined diplomacy as knowing how "to bring home the bacon without spilling the beans." As Jusserand's witty epigram suggests, the State Department's job—and that of every nation's foreign ministry—is a tough one. No matter how carefully foreign policymakers map out strategy, their calculations will always be thrown off by the random and unpredictable events of the real world—revolutions, assassinations, and nuclear explosions. They will never be able to anticipate completely the implications of proposed programs. For instance, American leaders could never have known that by rebuilding the shattered nation of Japan after World War II, they would help spawn a future economic competitor. All of this is merely to say that managing a nation's foreign affairs is an inexact science.

In spite of this undeniable fact, the Department of State has had a distinguished record during its 200-plus years of existence. Much of its success can be attributed to a tradition of exceptional leadership, a tradition that was established from the beginning. Of the first eight men who served as secretary of state, four went on to become president of the United States. During the 20th century, five department officials—four secretaries of state (Frank

Kellogg, Cordell Hull, George C. Marshall, and Henry Kissinger) and one department division head (Ralph Bunche)—have won the world's most respected award for diplomatic achievement, the Nobel Peace Prize. Whenever less accomplished secretaries have been at the helm, the career staff has been able to pick up the slack.

At almost every key moment in the nation's history, the State Department and its foreign arms—initially the consular and diplomatic services and more recently the Foreign Service—have made important contributions. During the revolutionary war, Benjamin Franklin and his fellow overseas diplomats obtained military and financial assistance without which the colonies would probably have been defeated by Great Britain. The first secretary of state, Thomas Jefferson, joined with President George Washington to establish the policy of neutrality—to which the nation largely adhered for more than a century—and helped the nation maintain this position while Europe descended

Ralph J. Bunche, right, is interviewed during a 1948 radio broadcast. Bunche had held various positions in the State Department before joining the UN Secretariat in 1949 where he was appointed principal secretary of the Palestine Commission. In 1950, he was awarded the Nobel Peace Prize for his role in the negotiations for an armistice agreement between Israel and the Arab states.

into the long nightmare of the Napoleonic Wars. When the War of 1812 temporarily tipped the United States from its isolationist perch, State Department representatives helped bring the conflict to a speedy conclusion. Meanwhile, American diplomats helped set the stage for internal development and westward expansion by negotiating treaties that enlarged the nation's territory and secured its borders. In subsequent years—as the department's influence temporarily waned—two secretaries of state still managed to have an enormous impact on foreign policy. During the 1820s, Secretary of State John Quincy Adams conceived the Monroe Doctrine, one of the most important policy statements in U.S. history, and during the 1860s, Secretary William Seward convinced Great Britain to stay out of the Civil War and negotiated the purchase of Alaska. In the wake of the Spanish-American War, as the United States began playing a greater role in international affairs, the State Department took on increasing importance. Strengthened in 1924 by the establishment of the Foreign Service, the department enjoyed its most productive years following World War II—helping establish the United Nations, developing containment policy, carrying out the Marshall Plan, and setting up the regional alliance system.

Under Presidents Johnson and Nixon, who claimed a great deal of foreign policy authority for themselves, the influence of the department again declined. But since 1972, the Department of State has been actively involved in many important policy issues—the strategic arms limitation talks, human rights, the fashioning of a strategy of counterterrorism, and the treaty returning the Panama Canal to Panamanian control.

Yet at the same time, the department's resources for influencing policy have been weakened. In the late 1970s, as international affairs became too technical to rely solely on the Department of State's Foreign Service, other cabinet-level departments—the Departments of Commerce and Agriculture—set up their own overseas arms. And in the late 1980s, the department has been threatened by cutbacks in staff and programs that could drastically reduce American influence abroad. One consequence is that the United States has fallen behind in paying its United Nations assessment. Under Article 19 of the UN Charter, the United States could lose its voting rights should it continue to fail to pay its dues within the next two or three years. Despite its senior rank in the cabinet, the cost of the State Department's operations at home and abroad amounts to only four-tenths of one percent of the federal budget. The cost of a single Trident submarine could pay the salaries and expenses for all State Department activities including more than 250 posts overseas, and there would still be money left over.

The UN General Assembly opens its 42nd annual session in September 1987. In recent years, the United States, which pays about a quarter of the international body's expenses, has fallen behind in paying its UN dues.

In part, the department's budgetary crisis is a symptom of one of its perennial handicaps: its lack of support among the voters. This problem differentiates it from its sister departments, such as the Department of Agriculture, which claims the interest of a large number of recipients of farm subsidies, and the Department of Health and Human Services, which commands support among the millions to whom it administers Social Security benefits. The Department of State's public services reach only a minority of voters directly, and even then, only on rare occasions.

Certain American attitudes also handicap the department in doing its job. Our traditional isolation has encouraged many of us to assume that the American way of doing things is the only way. Our phenomenally rapid growth as a nation has convinced many of us that all problems are solvable and has made us impatient for immediate results. It has often been left to the State Department—as the nation's eyes and ears abroad—to point out that we are just one of many strong nations in a disorderly world. As a consequence, this department has sometimes been a lightning rod for popular frustrations.

Since 1945, however, the American public's expectations have been lowered to a more realistic level. There is a growing realization that American goals are not universally shared and that our interests and those of our closest allies are not identical. The so-called bipolar world, centered on the duel between the superpowers, the Soviet Union and the United States, has given way to a multipolar world, with many centers of economic power, not only including Japan and West Germany, but also such nations as Brazil and Korea, which are now business competitors of the United States. The U.S. proportion of the world's gross national product has declined from 45 percent in 1945 to 20 percent today. At the same time, because of technological advancements, the world's nations have become increasingly interconnected.

In trying to understand recent changes in the global order, it is useful to consider the term *intermestic*, which was coined by the former dean of the Stanford University Law School, Bayless Manning, to describe subjects that are neither international nor domestic. According to Manning, classical international relations, which dealt with boundaries, national security, and the balance of powers, are being transformed. The new focus is more and more on economic matters: how to distribute trade, allocate resources, protect the environment, manage emerging technologies. All these intermestic issues cut across national borders. In such a setting, the State Department takes on a new importance. Although dwarfed in size and budget by nearly all other cabinet agencies, it possesses a unique fund of firsthand knowledge about the world outside our borders; experience in negotiating in international contexts; and special insight into the relationship between domestic interests and foreign policy. Emerging trends could give a fresh edge to the work of the department—the leading American presence overseas, often the initial point of contact with foreign peoples, and our nation's primary mechanism for understanding and influencing the rest of the world.

Department of State

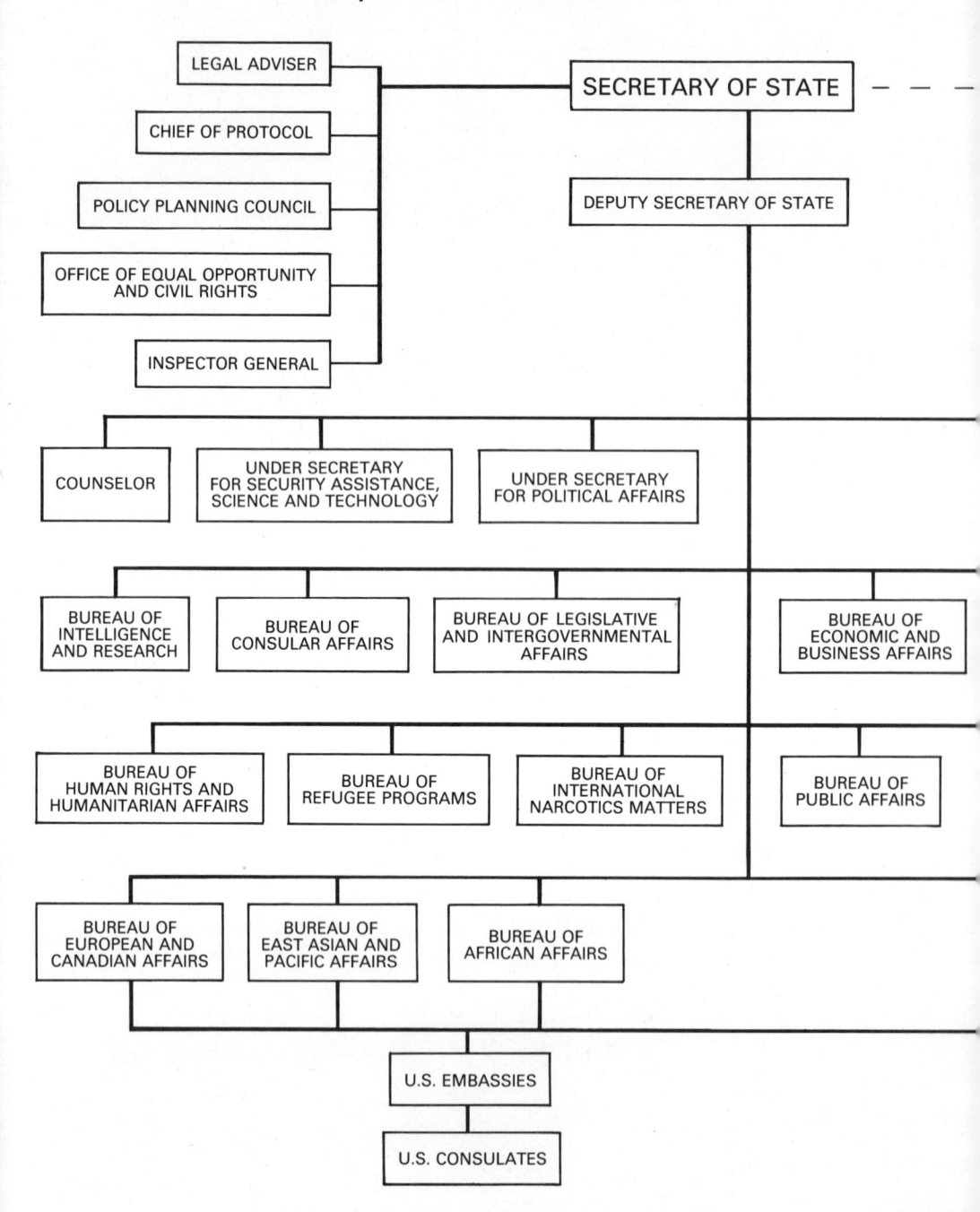

- SECRETARY OF STATE
  - LEGAL ADVISER
  - CHIEF OF PROTOCOL
  - POLICY PLANNING COUNCIL
  - OFFICE OF EQUAL OPPORTUNITY AND CIVIL RIGHTS
  - INSPECTOR GENERAL
  - DEPUTY SECRETARY OF STATE
    - COUNSELOR
    - UNDER SECRETARY FOR SECURITY ASSISTANCE, SCIENCE AND TECHNOLOGY
    - UNDER SECRETARY FOR POLITICAL AFFAIRS
      - BUREAU OF INTELLIGENCE AND RESEARCH
      - BUREAU OF CONSULAR AFFAIRS
      - BUREAU OF LEGISLATIVE AND INTERGOVERNMENTAL AFFAIRS
      - BUREAU OF ECONOMIC AND BUSINESS AFFAIRS
      - BUREAU OF HUMAN RIGHTS AND HUMANITARIAN AFFAIRS
      - BUREAU OF REFUGEE PROGRAMS
      - BUREAU OF INTERNATIONAL NARCOTICS MATTERS
      - BUREAU OF PUBLIC AFFAIRS
      - BUREAU OF EUROPEAN AND CANADIAN AFFAIRS
      - BUREAU OF EAST ASIAN AND PACIFIC AFFAIRS
      - BUREAU OF AFRICAN AFFAIRS
        - U.S. EMBASSIES
          - U.S. CONSULATES

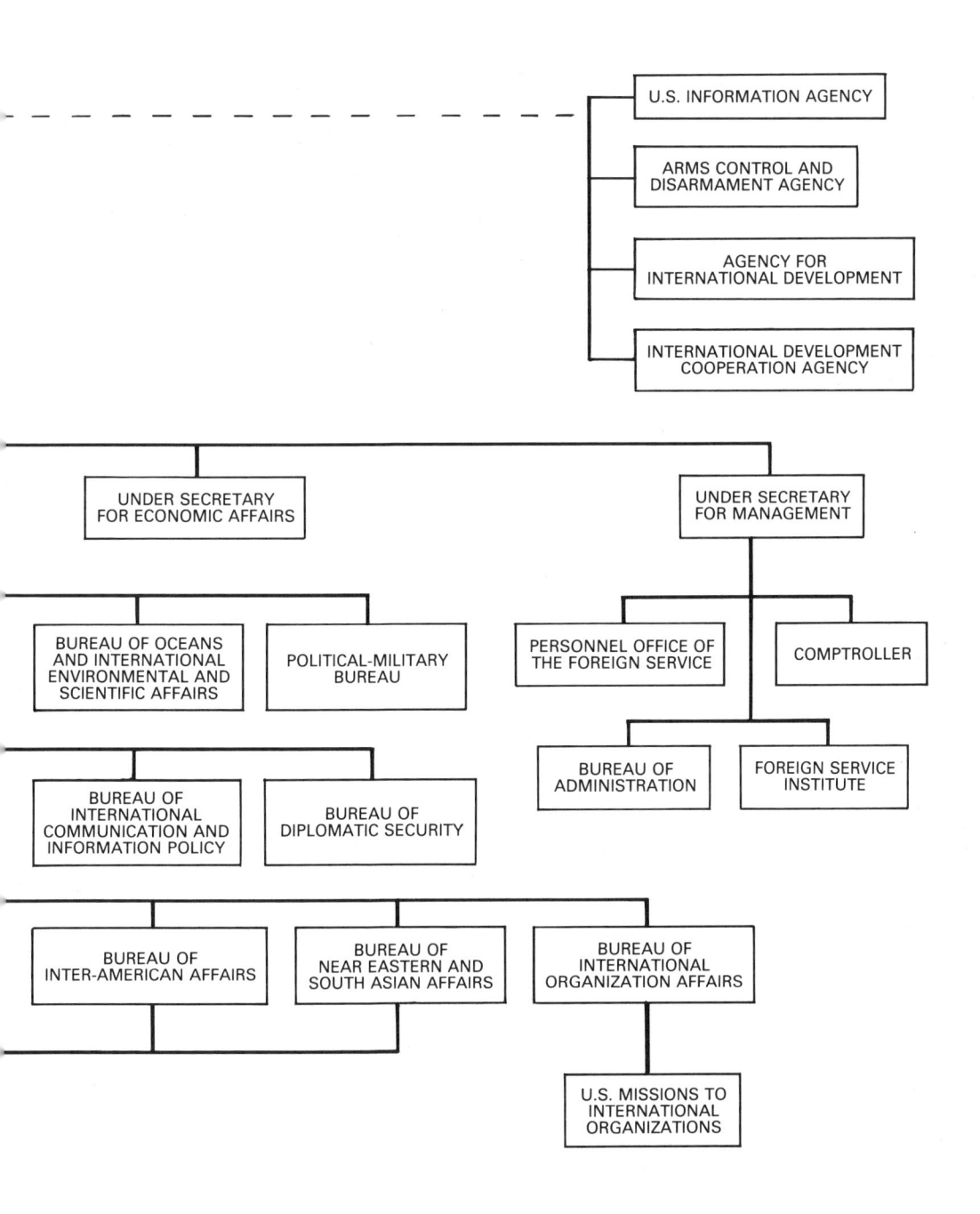

```
                                                    ┌── U.S. INFORMATION AGENCY
                                                    │
                                                    ├── ARMS CONTROL AND
– – – – – – – – – – – – – – – – – – – – – – – – – – ┤   DISARMAMENT AGENCY
                                                    │
                                                    ├── AGENCY FOR
                                                    │   INTERNATIONAL DEVELOPMENT
                                                    │
                                                    └── INTERNATIONAL DEVELOPMENT
                                                        COOPERATION AGENCY
```

- UNDER SECRETARY FOR ECONOMIC AFFAIRS
  - BUREAU OF OCEANS AND INTERNATIONAL ENVIRONMENTAL AND SCIENTIFIC AFFAIRS
  - POLITICAL-MILITARY BUREAU
  - BUREAU OF INTERNATIONAL COMMUNICATION AND INFORMATION POLICY
  - BUREAU OF DIPLOMATIC SECURITY
  - BUREAU OF INTER-AMERICAN AFFAIRS
  - BUREAU OF NEAR EASTERN AND SOUTH ASIAN AFFAIRS
  - BUREAU OF INTERNATIONAL ORGANIZATION AFFAIRS
    - U.S. MISSIONS TO INTERNATIONAL ORGANIZATIONS

- UNDER SECRETARY FOR MANAGEMENT
  - PERSONNEL OFFICE OF THE FOREIGN SERVICE
    - BUREAU OF ADMINISTRATION
    - FOREIGN SERVICE INSTITUTE
  - COMPTROLLER

GLOSSARY

Alliance An agreement between two or more nations to join together in defense of their common interests.

Attaché A technical specialist who functions as an official with diplomatic rank and who is attached to an embassy or foreign mission.

Cabinet An advisory group selected by the president to aid him in making decisions.

Civil Service The administration service of a government or international agency exclusive of the armed forces in which appointments are determined by a competitive examination or through a merit system.

Consul An official appointed by a government to reside in a foreign country in order to assist citizens of the appointing state and advance their commercial interests.

Containment A foreign policy adopted by the Truman administration aimed at containing communist power within its existing boundaries and preventing the industrial or emerging powers of Europe or the Middle East from falling under the control of the Soviet Union.

Détente A French diplomatic term that describes an easing of tensions between two or more countries, generally used to describe the relationship the United States had with the Soviet Union and the People's Republic of China during the 1970s.

Dissent Channel A system that enables State Department officials to formally express opposition to American foreign policy by sending a memo to the department headquarters in Washington, D.C.

Embassy A body of diplomatic representation consisting of an ambassador and the ambassador's staff. Unlike consulates, which under the direction of embassies focus on providing assistance to Americans living in or visiting their districts, embassies concentrate on government-to-government relations between the United States and foreign nations.

Expansionism The policy or practice of territorial expansion by a nation, often with the goal of increasing foreign trade or colonial holdings.

Isolationism The theory and practice of noninvolvement in affairs of other nations, used to describe U.S. policy toward Europe before World War I.

Military Assistance Advisory Group (MAAG) An extension of the Department of Defense that administers American military assistance to foreign nations and provides combat training.

Neutrality The legal status of a nation that does not participate in a war between other nations.

Protectorate The relationship of superior authority assumed by one nation over a dependent one.

Spoils System The awarding of government jobs to political supporters and friends.

Tariff A tax levied on imports to help protect a nation's industry, business, labor, and agriculture from foreign competition or to raise revenue.

Terrorism Actions undertaken by governments, individuals, or groups using violence or threats of violence for political purposes.

SELECTED REFERENCES

Acheson, Dean. *Present at the Creation.* New York: Norton, 1969.

Blancké, W. Wendell. *The Foreign Service of the United States.* New York: Praeger, 1969.

DeConde, Alexander. *The American Secretary of State.* New York: Praeger, 1963.

Estes, Thomas S., and E. Allan Lightner, Jr. *The Department of State.* New York: Praeger, 1976.

Hartmann, Frederick H. *The New Age of American Foreign Policy.* New York: Macmillan, 1970.

Mayer, Martin. *The Diplomats.* New York: Doubleday, 1983.

Nixon, Richard. *U.S. Foreign Policy for the 1970s: A Report to the Congress.* 3 vols. Washington, D.C.: Government Printing Office, 1971.

Price, Don K., ed. *The Secretary of State.* Englewood Cliffs, NJ: Prentice-Hall in association with the American Assembly, Columbia University, 1960.

Simpson, Smith. *Anatomy of the State Department.* Boston: Houghton Mifflin, 1967.

Steigman, Andrew L. *The Foreign Service of the United States: First Line of Defense.* Boulder, CO: Westview, 1985.

Stuart, Graham H. *The Department of State.* New York: Macmillan, 1949.

Trask, David. *A Short History of the U.S. Department of State, 1781–1981.* Washington, D.C.: Department of State, 1981.

INDEX

Accounts, Bureau of, 42
Acheson, Dean, 60–61
Adams, John, 21, 30
Adams, John Quincy, 31–34, 38, 107
Adams-Onís Treaty, 33
Administration, Bureau of, 72, 88
African Affairs, Bureau of, 72, 76
Agency for International Development, 72, 75–76, 101
Alaska, 41, 107
Archives, Laws, and Commissions, Bureau of, 38
Arms Control and Disarmament Agency, 72
Articles of Confederation, 24
Atlantic Ocean, 22

Begin, Menachem, 65
Blaine, James G., 43–44
Bonaparte, Napoleon, 29–31, 37
Bryan, William Jennings, 50–52
Bunche, Ralph, 66
Byrnes, James F., 55

Camp David Accords, 65
Carter, Jimmy, 60, 65, 67–68
Central Treaty Organization (CENTO), 60
China, 38, 47, 61, 63, 77
Christopher, Warren, 68
Civil Service League, 42
Civil War, 40–41, 107
Clay, Henry, 31, 38
Cleveland, Grover, 44
Commerce, Department of, 101
Congress, U.S., 24–25, 29, 33, 38, 44, 49–50, 52, 55, 57, 63, 65, 69

Constitution, U.S., 24
Consular Affairs, Bureau of, 72, 79
Consular Bureau, 38, 42
Consulates, 16–17, 21, 23, 28, 38, 41, 49–50, 53, 72, 94
Containment, 56, 59
Continental Congress, 20–23
Country teams, 94
Cuba, 44–45

Deane, Silas, 21
Declaration of Independence, 15, 21, 25
Defense, Department of, 16, 81–82, 101
   Military Assistance Advisory Groups, 101
Department of Foreign Affairs (DFA), 21, 23–24
Détente, 63
Dewey, William, 44
Diplomatic Bureau, 38, 42
Diplomatic Security, Bureau of, 72, 87–88, 98
Disbursing, Bureau of, 38
Division of Information, 49
Douglass, Frederick, 66
Dulles, John Foster, 16, 60–61

East Asian and Pacific Affairs, Bureau of, 72, 76
Economic and Business Affairs, Bureau of, 72, 82
Economic Cooperation Administration, 57
Economic Warfare, Board of, 55
Eisenhower, Dwight D., 16, 60
Embassies, 16–17, 72, 93–94, 100, 101
   administrative section, 97–99

consular section, 99–100
economic section, 95–97
political section, 95
European and Canadian Affairs, Bureau of, 72, 76

First Pan-American Conference, 43
Fish, Hamilton, 42, 49
Florida, 22, 30, 33
Foreign Affairs, Committee on, 20–21
Foreign Agricultural Service, 101
Foreign Commercial Service, 101
Foreign Fund, 28
Foreign Service, 62, 72, 102, 107
  definition of, 16
  embassies and, 95
  entrance examination, 89
  establishment of, 52–54
  reorganization of, 55, 65
Foreign Service Act of 1946, 55
Foreign Service Act of 1980, 65
France, 19–22, 29–31, 34, 40–41, 47, 62, 77
Franklin, Benjamin, 106
Franz Ferdinand, archduke of Austria, 50
French Revolution, 26–27, 29

Germany, 20, 47, 50–52
Ghent, Treaty of, 32
Grant, Ulysses S., 42
Great Britain, 19–23, 29–35, 40, 44, 47–48, 50–51, 77, 106
Great Lakes, 22, 31
Great Seal of the United States, 15–16
Guadalupe Hidalgo, Treaty of, 40

Hawley-Smoot Tariff of 1930, 55
Hay, John, 45, 47–48
Hearst, William Randolph, 44
Herter, Christian, 57, 60

Home Bureau, 38
House, Edward M., 52
Hughes, Charles Evans, 52
Hull, Cordell, 54–55, 106
Human Rights and Humanitarian Affairs, Bureau of, 72, 83–84

Indexes and Archives, Bureau of, 42
Intelligence and Research, Bureau of, 72, 79
Inter-American Affairs, Bureau of, 72, 76
Interior, Department of the, 41
International Communication and Information Policy, Bureau of, 72, 85–87
International Development Cooperation Agency, 65, 72, 75–76
International Narcotics Matters, Bureau of, 72, 85
International Organization Affairs, Bureau of, 72, 76–77
Iran, 67–68, 73

Jackson, Andrew, 32–33, 38
Jay, John, 21, 23, 26, 29
Jay's Treaty, 29
Jefferson, Thomas, 15, 25–31, 106
Johnson, Andrew, 40–41
Johnson, Lyndon, 109
Jusserand, Jules, 105

Kellogg, Frank, 52, 106
Kennan, George, 56
Kirkpatrick, Jeane, 77
Kissinger, Henry, 63, 65, 106
Knox, Philander C., 49

Lansing, Robert, 52
Latin America, 34–35, 38, 43, 47, 59, 69, 77

Laurens, Henry, 20–21
Legislative and Intergovernmental Affairs, Bureau of, 72, 78–79
Libya, 69
Lincoln, Abraham, 40
Livingston, Robert R., 21, 23, 31
Lodge, Henry Cabot, 42
Louisiana Purchase, 30–31
Lusitania, 51–52

McCarthy, Joseph, 17, 61–62
McLane, Louis, 38
Madison, James, 31
Maine, 44
Manning, Bayless, 109
Mao Zedong, 61
Marcos, Ferdinand, 74
Marshall, George, 16, 56–57, 60
Marshall Plan, 56–58, 106–7
Mein, John Gordon, 67
Mercantile imperialism, 43
Mexican-American War, 39–40
Mississippi River, 22, 30, 33
Monroe, James, 31–32, 34
Monroe Doctrine, 33–34, 40, 43–44, 47, 107
Mortefontaine, Treaty of, 30
Muskie, Edmund, 68

Narcotics Matters, Bureau of, 72
National Security Act of 1947, 17, 60
National Security Council, 17, 60
Near Eastern and South Asian Affairs, Bureau of, 72, 76
Neutrality Act of 1794, 29
Neutrality Proclamation, 28–29, 34
Newfoundland, 22
New Orleans, Battle of, 32
Nicaragua, 69
Nixon, Richard M., 16–17, 60, 63, 107

North Atlantic Treaty Organization (NATO), 20, 59

Oceans and International Environmental and Scientific Affairs, Bureau of, 72, 83
Office of Equal Opportunity and Civil Rights, 72, 88–89
Open Door Policy, 48
Opium Wars, 47–48

Pacheco, Romualdo, 66
Paine, Thomas, 20
Pardons, Remissions, Copyrights, and Library, Bureau of, 38
Paris, France, 20, 25, 45, 52
Paris Peace Pact, 52
Paris, Treaty of, 22, 29
Pendleton Act, 42
Philadelphia, Pennsylvania, 20, 24, 28
Pierce, Franklin, 41
Pinckney, Thomas, 30
Policy Planning Council, 72, 74–75
Political-Military Bureau, 72, 81–82
Polk, James, 39–40
Public Affairs, Bureau of, 16, 72, 80–81
Pulitzer, Joseph, 44

Qaddafi, Muammar, 69

Randolph, John, 38
Reagan, Ronald, 60, 68–69, 73
Refugee Programs, Bureau of, 72, 85
Reign of Terror, 27
Revolutionary war, 20–21, 29
Rio Pact, 59
Robespierre, Maximilien, 27
Rogers Act, 52–54
Rogers, John Jacob, 52–53
Rogers, William P., 16

Roosevelt, Franklin, 54–56
Roosevelt, Theodore, 42, 44, 47, 49–50, 53
Root, Elihu, 46
Russia, 20, 32, 34, 38, 41, 47

Sadat, Anwar, 65
Scott, Winfield, 39
Seminole Indians, 33
Senior Foreign Service (SFS), 65
Seward, William, 40–41, 107
Shultz, George, 73
Sofaer, Abraham, 73–74
Southeast Asia Treaty Organization (SEATO), 59–60
Soviet Union, 56, 61, 63, 68–69, 74, 77, 109
Spain, 19–21, 29–30, 33–34, 44
Spanish-American War, 44–45, 47, 107
Special agents, 28
Spoils system, 38, 42, 49
Stalin, Joseph, 56
Stanton, Benjamin, 37
State, Department of,
  budget for, 17, 28, 37, 41, 49, 107
  comptroller, 72, 88
  containment policy, 56
  creation of, 21–25
  creation of Foreign Service, 52–54
  domestic responsibilities of, 25, 41
  foreign alliances and, 59–60
  Foreign Service nationals, 103
  functional bureaus, 78–88
  history to 1823, 20–35
  hierarchy of, 71–73
  inspector-general, 72, 88–89
  legal adviser, 72, 73, 74
  minority employment in, 65–66, 88–89
  organization of, 71–91
  policy of neutrality and, 28–30, 33–34, 37, 50, 106

recognition of foreign governments, 27, 94
regional bureaus, 77–78
reorganization, 38, 41–42, 49–50
Stettinius, Edward, Jr., 55
Strategic Arms Limitations Talks, 63
Strategic Services, Office of, 55

Taft, William Howard, 49–50, 53
Terrorism, 17, 66–69
Trade Agreements Act of 1934, 55
Translating and Miscellaneous Bureau, 38
Treasury, Department of, 49
Trist, Nicholas P., 39–40
Truman, Harry, 16, 56–57, 59–60
Truman Doctrine, 56

United Nations, 16, 55, 59–60, 77, 107
U.S. Foreign Policy for the 1970s (Nixon and Kissinger), 63
U.S. Information Agency, 65, 72, 75–76, 100–101
U.S. Information Service, 100–101

Vance, Cyrus, 61, 68
Vandenberg, Arthur H., 57, 59
Vergennes, Comte de, 22
Versailles, Treaty of, 52
Vietnam War, 62, 75

War Information, Office of, 55
War of 1812, 31–32, 107
Washburne, Elihu, 42
Washington, George, 24, 27–28, 30, 34, 106
Wharton, Clifford R., 66
Willis, Francis, 66
Wilson, Woodrow, 16, 27, 50–52
World War I, 47, 50, 57
World War II, 55–57, 65, 107

Young, Andrew, 77

Carl F. Bartz is a retired American diplomat who formerly held assignments overseas with the Department of State, the Department of Defense, and the U.S. Information Agency. He received his B.A. from Harvard College and his Ph.D. in history and politics from the University of California. During World War II he served as a Japanese-language officer in the U.S. Navy. As a diplomat, he was stationed at American embassies in Japan, Korea, Burma, and Pakistan. Among his previous publications are *Washington Embassies: A Guide for the Private Sector* and *Operating Internationally*.

Arthur M. Schlesinger, jr., served in the White House as special assistant to Presidents Kennedy and Johnson. He is the author of numerous works in American history and has twice been awarded the Pulitzer Prize. He taught history at Harvard College for many years and is currently Albert Schweitzer Professor of the Humanities at the City College of New York.

PICTURE CREDITS:

Agency for International Development: p. 75; AP/Wide World Photos: pp. 63, 73, 77, 84; The Bettmann Archive: pp. 36, 43, 51; Black Star Photo: cover (top); Drug Enforcement Agency: p. 86; Michael Evans, The White House: p. 70; Library of Congress: pp. 18, 22, 23, 25, 26, 27, 28, 32, 34, 39, 40, 45, 48, 53, 54, 58; National Archives: pp. 46, 59; Peace Corps: p. 102; Pete Souza, The White House: p. 2; Reuters/Bettmann Newsphotos: p. 95; State Department Magazine: pp. 66, 90, 95, 98, 100; Sygma Photos: cover (right); UN Photo: p. 108; Uniphoto: cover (left); UPI/Bettmann Newsphotos: pp. 17, 61, 62, 64, 67, 68, 78, 81, 87, 98, 106; U.S. Department of State: pp. 14, 80, 92; The White House: p. 104.

JX
1706
.A4
1989a

14.95

JX
1706
.A4
1989a